HER HEART BEATS FOR ANCIENT BEASTS

Books by Calvin Demmer

Short Story Collections
The Sea Was a Fair Master
Dark Celebrations
The Town That Feared Dusk
Her Heart Beats for Ancient Beasts
Through the Ravenous Night We Ride

HER HEART BEATS FOR ANCIENT BEASTS

CALVIN DEMMER

TABLE OF CONTENTS

HIGHWAY HUNGER

It couldn't be alive?

It *was.*

Dudley Ellington couldn't see the animal's face, but based on the tufts of bloody fur, he thought it might be a rat or a squirrel. He stepped closer, and the creature's legs shook as if it were attempting to kick-start its body back to life.

Its movements ceased.

Dudley looked around, and all he saw was the long, empty stretch of highway. Why was there never a good stick lying around when you needed one? He tapped his boot on the animal, hoping for a response. He got nothing. Were his eyes playing tricks? He thought its legs moved a moment ago.

He tapped the animal again.

This time, one of its arms stretched out and then down, as if it were trying to push the button to answer a question on a game show. Dudley stepped back—not out of fear, as he assured himself, but to get a better view.

The paw jiggled.

"Yo, Felipe. Come check this out." Dudley ran his hand over his slicked-back hair. He looked to the white pickup when he got no reply from his coworker.

Felipe sat in the front seat with his orange helmet covering his eyes.

"Felipe, wake up."

Felipe groaned, slowly pushing open the driver-side door. "What's it now, Dud? I told you we can always take an extra thirty minutes for lunch. I was just about to get some rest. No one will give a shit."

"There's something on the road. I was gonna scoop it up, but it must be alive."

Felipe's eyes widened. He climbed out of the vehicle and marched to Dudley.

"Get back," he said as he passed Dudley.

Dudley did as instructed, oddly reassured by the sudden authority in his coworker's voice. Felipe would surely help the critter, maybe take it somewhere for injured animals. He was still new to the job and wasn't sure of the correct protocol.

Felipe hovered over the creature. "It's a squirrel. At least, it was. Half its body has been smashed."

"Damn."

"Yeah, it's a bummer for sure. But there's nothing we can do. Best leave it be and let it die in peace."

"Leave it be? It's in pain."

"That's right. We leave it. It's not dead, and we only collect the dead."

Dudley stepped forward. "What about the injured animals? Where do you take them?"

"Injured animals." Felipe scoffed, staring at the road. "Dud. Now isn't the time for this. Let it go."

The squirrel twitched, and Dudley imagined it hearing them talk about how they would simply desert it. That was nonsense, of course, as squirrels couldn't understand humans, but still, he couldn't allow it to suffer. He would have to put it out of its misery.

Dudley raised his boot, telling himself this was the most merciful thing he could do.

"No!" Felipe shouted, tackling him to the ground.

"What the fuck, man?" Dudley pushed Felipe off before getting to his feet and dusting his pants, not sure how much good it would do as they already had a stain or two from the takeaway burger he'd devoured for lunch. "Why would—"

"Dud. You need to listen to me." Felipe glanced around. "We need to get going. I can explain everything once we're on the move."

* * *

Dudley sat next to Felipe as the vehicle growled along the stretch of blacktop. The poor animal had long since vanished in the rearview mirror, and he was still waiting for his coworker to shed some light on his peculiar behavior. Why did he always find himself in these weird situations? On second thought, he knew. He had asked for this one in particular.

Less than six months ago, he had driven home after having a few beers at his favorite pub. A youngster on a BMX with no lights had been crossing a road. Dudley's reaction time had been too slow to prevent the impact. Luckily, the kid only suffered a broken arm. Unluckily, the story blew up in the town, causing Dudley to lose his job as a sales assistant at the hardware store. At least he had escaped jail time, but the fine and community service—disposing of roadkill—sucked all the same.

Felipe drummed his fingers on the steering wheel; his eyes narrowed on the road ahead. "I didn't think we'd see something dying on the road so soon, Dud. I should've known better, especially with this damn highway. This road is like either a snack platter or a buffet for it. Take your pick. I should've told you sooner, no doubt about it, but once you hear what I have to say, you'll understand."

Empty seconds ticked by.

"What happened back there? I want to know, now," Dudley pressed him.

Felipe cleared his throat a few times, but no words followed. He appeared rattled, which was unlike the man Dudley had come to know the last two weeks. So, Dudley tapped his fingers on his thigh and forced himself to wait for Felipe to explain.

Felipe slowed the vehicle, checking the side mirrors. "You're going to think I'm fucking nuts, but I've seen it."

"Seen what? Why'd you act so damn weird back there?" Dudley asked, unable to hold back any longer.

"Well, some people call it by a specific name, something creepy, but that's too long and hard to remember. I call it the Road Demon."

"Huh? What are you—"

"Listen, Dud. There is this … thing. It feeds off the injured, the dying, and you don't want to get in its way. It was coming for the animal. I sensed it. You're never the same after you see it, feel it, and connect with it. It showed me something after getting into my mind."

"Felipe. I'm not—"

"It looks like a squid, or a jellyfish with eyes, or something like that, at least at first. This thing rides the road as if it's a boat cruising on water. When I saw it, it changed, transformed rather, until it looked like the red truck that crashed into my son's car and killed him years ago. I swear there was even blood on its grill. It amplified all the sorrow and all the pain, like I was back in the moment when I arrived at the accident site. It was hard to look away. It was hard to get away."

"I'm sorry about your son, Felipe, but I don't know what the hell you—"

"Dud, Dud, Dud." Felipe shook his head. "The people who work on the roads here—the cops and other emergency services and so on—all know about it. They all respect it. You can't go breaking the rules. Not even if you're new. That could get you killed, but it could also create trouble for all of us. We don't know this thing's full capabilities. It's best to not stir trouble. Let it be."

Dudley shrugged. The atmosphere around him had contracted, like paper crushed into a ball by a fist, but he braced against it. He wouldn't be fooled. This had to be a strange hazing Felipe put him through. Scare him a bit so they could joke about it later over a few cold ones.

"So," Felipe continued, "first things first. We never pick up the wounded or suffering, only the dead."

"Wait. What about people?" Dudley yanked his security vest away from his neck because the fabric agitated his skin.

"Ahhh, well, that's more complicated. If I see people, I get away and call the emergency services. Let them decide what to do. It's—"

"You wouldn't help someone injured on the side of the road?" Dudley's stomach knotted.

"Some people place wounded animals near the road—stuff like rats or chickens. They hope the Road Demon will take the animals as sacrifices and leave people be. A lot of people believe it causes some of the traffic accidents, especially when it's hungry."

"Do you believe that?"

"Like I said, it's complicated. I choose to stay as uninvolved as possible."

"Where does this 'Road Demon' come from?"

Felipe licked his bottom lip. "Man. Now, that's a good question. I've heard all sorts of stories, from it being a revengeful trucker back from the dead as some sea-creature ghost, to it being a demon that escaped from hell. I've even heard it's an alien that fell from the sky. Truth is no one knows. It's always been here."

"Felipe. This better be some dumbass joke, and it still isn't a good excuse for leaving that little guy to suffer. I'm not some idiot—"

"Shit!" Felipe said, slamming the brakes.

Dudley looked ahead to see a deer disappear under the front of the pickup. A loud *thud* came, and the vehicle jerked to the left. Felipe cursed again, fighting the steering wheel.

The pickup stopped on the dirt alongside the road.

Dudley opened his door and jumped out, ignoring the sharp pain in his neck.

"Wait," Felipe said, rubbing his own left shoulder.

Dudley didn't obey. Instead, he walked a few steps, until he could see the wounds on the animal. A stab of guilt shot through his core. The poor deer... It was a brutal way to go, except... Its leg flinched.

It was still alive.

This couldn't be happening again.

Dudley stood still less than three yards from the animal, hearing footsteps approach from behind him. A hand patted his shoulder. He heard Felipe`s voice.

"Come on, Dud. The vehicle's okay. We got to go. We've been through this. Let it be."

Dudley, transfixed, couldn't move. He couldn't even turn to face his coworker, as his head felt stuck in place. The guilt ate at him, severing his ability to move. He needed to escape the feeling's claim for control. He wasn't the driver, but even if he had been, there was nothing that could've altered the accident. It had gone down too fast. And now he couldn't avert his gaze from the animal before him.

Trees rustled in the distance.

A cool wind washed over him.

Felipe tugged on him, but Dudley refused to budge. "Dud. We gotta go. It's coming for the deer."

The road ahead of Dudley appeared to sway slightly, from side to side, but that couldn't be; it must've been an optical illusion. Maybe he was in shock from the accident? He focused, noticing a strange dark-gray bump, about seven feet in height, on the surface of the road. It was coming closer, coming for them. It shared the same color as the asphalt as though part of it, yet the road didn't crack and break. Maybe the bump replicated the color of the road, like a chameleon? Maybe the bump was like a ghost or apparition, and thus didn't affect the asphalt?

Except it wasn't a bump.

It was a head.

Two large eyes with U-shaped pupils stared at him. The head was similar in shape to that of an old lightbulb. An octopus? The head definitely belonged to something from the *Cephalopoda* class. Dudley glanced down, believing he saw spectral tentacles attached to the head; the tentacles appeared to reach back into the road.

The octopus-like head shimmered, then transformed into a pack of rats rumbling over each other in a ball. Dudley gasped; he had loathed the vile vermin ever since he'd gone down to the basement one day as a kid. He had called for his mother but got no response. By the time his foot had touched the bottom step, he'd seen his mother's body lying inert in the corner, near the beat-up washing machine. Focusing, he had realized it wasn't shadows over her but a pile of filthy fucking rats. They gnawed away at her as if she were a feast spread out for them.

Dudley had grabbed a broom, but by the time he'd scared away his foe it was already too late. His mother was dead. He would later learn she had tripped, damaging her spinal cord. She had been alive, unable to move, when the rats came out for their snack. That frigid, heart-crushing fear and sorrow resurfaced within him as if he were a child all over again. Tears built up in his eyes.

"Dudley, come on!" Felipe commanded from behind him.

His coworker had been telling the truth. He had to escape. He needed to look away.

Felipe tugged on him. "We've got to fucking go."

There were no other vehicles, the light had dimmed, and the air was thinner. Dudley stepped back. The rats transformed back to the octopus head. It increased its speed, now rampaging toward them like a rogue elephant busting its way through the jungle. Dudley willed movement upon himself.

He turned around and ran.

Felipe, ahead of him, slid into the pickup.

The engine roared.

"Hurry up!" Felipe shouted over the noise.

Dudley hopped into the vehicle, and Felipe didn't waste a second pulling away. Looking back, Dudley saw strange black tendrils shoot out of the road into the air. They fell around the deer.

"What the fuck?" he said.

"I told you. I fucking told you." Felipe shook his head.

The deer moved, rising into the air as if a magician levitated it. The tendrils solidified in shape, appearing to be tentacles now. They wrapped around the animal, then tightened with such force that whatever bones weren't broken by the crash were shattered now. Blood spurted out from the deer's wounds and orifices. The animal started to spin, around and around, faster and faster, like meat on a malfunctioning rotisserie. The tentacles worked their prey with an educated ease, and then the deer—what remained of it—hit the ground.

The octopus head and its array of cephalopod-like limbs retreated into the road. Gone, as if they had never existed. A paralyzing fear lingered beneath Dudley's skin, vacating his pores slowly, unmercifully.

"Hey. Snap out of it," Felipe said.

"What the fuck just happened? What did I see?" Dudley turned to face Felipe.

Felipe's gaze stayed focused ahead. "The Road Demon."

"We got to do something, tell someone."

"Haven't you been listening? Everyone who matters already knows about it. There's nothing to be done. We let it be."

Dudley's body was numb. The mixture of emotions swirling in his gut was a debilitating cocktail, stronger than moonshine he had once drunk at his uncle's place. He dropped his gaze, unsure what to do, unsure what to say.

"You'll feel better tomorrow. You escaped its mind games, at least this time," Felipe said. "I struggled the same the first time I saw it, and I didn't have anyone to warn me. It takes a bit out of you, I know. But you have a strong mind, Dud. Most people cave the first time they see it... Anyway, we're finished early for today. Let's go straight to my place. You can take the pickup and get me in the morning. Cool?"

Dudley nodded. What else could he do? His world would never be the same again. He cursed himself internally for knocking the kid on the bike. Why couldn't his life have taken a smooth and *normal* path? Maybe his cousin would know of work far, far away from long stretches of road? It would be worth giving him a call once Dudley completed his hell known as community service.

"Everything is going to be fine, Dud."

"What did it do to the deer?" Dudley asked, surprising himself. Deep down, he already knew the answer. He was thankful he could still talk, and hearing his own voice helped calm the electric sensation shooting up and down his legs.

"It ate the deer. Well, in its way. It's like it squeezes out whatever life is left in its victim, leaving nothing but a pale bag of broken bones and shredded flesh. You'll see when we retrieve the carcass tomorrow, if it's still there. Fucking nasty, but like I said, you get used to it. You'll learn to let it be. If you want to live, that is."

"Crazy, crazy shit," Dudley mumbled.

* * *

Dudley put on his safety vest over a long-sleeved shirt and grabbed his lunch box. He hadn't slept much, as the image of the evil entity crushing the life out of the deer kept popping into the fore of his mind.

He exited his apartment and climbed into the pickup.

Thankfully, Felipe had cleaned off any blood and bits from the front of the vehicle when they got to his place the previous day. Felipe had even invited him in and offered him a beer, which Dudley had accepted. His coworker had been right; he did feel a bit better today, so long as he didn't linger on the strange memories of yesterday.

Still early to go to Felipe's, Dudley convinced himself to drive a section of the highway. He wanted only to drive and for nothing weird to happen. He needed nothing weird to happen.

Gray clouds smothered the sky above the highway. For a moment, Dudley wondered if it wasn't some augur of dangerous highway travel; but as he carried on, the early morning sun broke through the haze. He eased his foot off the accelerator, ignoring the occasional vehicle honking at him. His mind eased, and time didn't feel like its usual tick-tock countdown. Tranquility took control, eventually reigning supreme.

In the side mirror, there were no more vehicles.

In the distance, a white minivan sat alongside the road.

Dudley parked behind the vehicle. A rear tire appeared flat and one of the back doors was open. He sighed, accepting he had to get out, and opened his driver-side door.

He strolled to the van, half expecting a bunch of kids in soccer uniforms to burst out.

"Hello, is anyone here?"

The driver-side door opened, and a bloodied hand with long blue nails reached outward.

"Help me," a female voice whimpered. "I'm injured. My phone doesn't work."

Dudley opened the door farther. A young woman was leaning over, trying to crawl out of the vehicle.

"Ah, wait," Dudley said, deciding it best for her not to exit into the road. He jogged around the vehicle and opened the passenger door.

"This side." He reached in to help her.

A golf-ball-sized bruise swelled above her right eye. Blood stained her nostrils and most of her frilly-collared white shirt. She stepped out and limped forward.

"Please," she said, "you've got to help me. He rammed me off the road."

"Of course. Can you walk to my pickup?" The fear of the Road Demon surfaced in Dudley's mind, creating a sensation of burning ants scurrying up his back. He remembered Felipe's words, "Let it be," but he couldn't abandon the woman. Plus, she wasn't technically on the road.

"Yes. I can walk."

"Good. Let's get out of here."

Dudley led the woman to his vehicle, giving her a hand when she stumbled by the passenger door. Before she could get in, an engine growled behind them; the woman looked back and screamed.

"It's him! It's him!" she shouted.

Dudley turned around, expecting the worst, but all that approached was a black Cadillac.

The car stopped about twenty yards from them.

"That's the man who hit me." The woman jumped into the pickup and locked the door.

Dudley didn't move. There could be nothing worse than the evil entity he had borne witness to on the road. This was simply a man. He could handle him.

The Cadillac's door opened, and the driver got out but remained standing behind the door. "I can't believe that bitch survived. She cut me off earlier, but I showed her." He grinned.

"Listen, I don't want any trouble. I'm taking her to the hospital." Dudley had already memorized the license plate number and was looking over the man to prepare a police description. Unfortunately, apart from the dyed blond hair, nothing unique stood out about him. He was of average height, wore jeans and a blue-gray checkered shirt, and had a smile no more special than that of a movie extra.

"No trouble, you say. I'm afraid that isn't a possibility." The man slammed the door closed and strolled forward, revealing a baseball bat.

Dudley considered retreating to the pickup; the man sprinted for him.

Dudley ducked under the first swing of the bat. He weaved away from the second. Before his attacker could take another swipe, he stepped to the man and grabbed his arms.

His foe wriggled like an animal caught in a trap and, after breaking free, created enough space for another strike.

The bat bashed Dudley in the back, and he winced while trying to move away. He heard the pickup start, but he resisted the urge to shout for the woman not to leave him behind. He leapt backward instead, expecting another hit, but the man had turned his attention to the woman.

"You're going nowhere, bitch." He marched toward her, lifting the bat for a swing.

The woman drove straight at the man and knocked him down, riding over his left leg in the process. A loud *crack* echoed as tire met bone. The man screamed as he rolled away.

The woman cut the engine and stepped out, ignoring her assailant.

He lay on the ground, cursing her with every foul word Dudley had ever heard.

"I'm going to call the cops now." The woman held up Dudley's cell phone.

Dudley, who was catching his breath, didn't respond. He surveyed the road around them, surprised no other vehicle had come by yet, and then he saw it. The asphalt swayed, more violently than before—this time it danced like a broken electric cable seeking a victim to strike. The wind had picked up, and its cold touch caressed his skin.

"We have to go," he said.

"Go? The cops will be here soon," the woman replied.

"We can't wait." Dudley moved to the man on the ground and tried to grab his hands. "I want to help you. We need to get you away, to a hospital."

"Don't touch me." The man groped for his bat, but it was too far away. "I'm not going anywhere with you fucks. You're both dead. Do you hear me?"

Dudley studied the road. The ghostly octopus-like head rose out of the asphalt. The Road Demon's eyes narrowed as its speed toward them increased. Shades of red and black swirled within its being, and its tentacles spread all around it, curling at the ends like hooks.

A wave of disorientation washed over Dudley. His eyes itched as memories from his life played in his mind. Was the Road Demon searching for something to use on him? Dudley pictured his father when he had cancer, then he immediately fought back with a memory of his father buying him his first bike. The Road Demon reached for a memory of Dudley's uncle, who had been murdered at an ATM, but Dudley countered with thoughts of his uncle playing guitar and singing for the family.

"No," Dudley muttered, bracing against the feeling of a million tentacles swimming inside his brain.

Blood dripped from his nostrils.

His hands clenched into fists.

"Fuck you!" Dudley screamed and looked away. His eyes, lungs and skin felt on fire, but the crushing sensation eased on his brain.

He ran to the woman and yanked her by the arm. "Let's go!"

She mumbled in protest but followed him and hopped into the vehicle. "You can't leave him there to get away with what he's done! He would have killed me!"

"He won't get away."

"He *will*. He can still crawl to his car. I want to see the cops arrest him."

Behind the wheel, Dudley hit the gas, not interested in what the woman wanted. His eyes remained locked on the road ahead. His only goal was to get as far away from the Road Demon as possible.

"I can't believe we're leaving him! If he gets away, I'll report you too. It doesn't matter that you helped me." The woman craned her neck to see her attacker.

"For fuck's sake. It's coming for him, and we can't help him!" Dudley said. "There's no time. It's not our fault. We have to let it be. You can't beat it."

"What's not our... What the—?" The woman's voice cracked as she stared through the rear windshield. "The man... He lifted off the ground. There's black stuff all around him. What is going on?"

"I told you it was coming. But...but everything will be all right." It was all Dudley could think of saying, repeating Felipe's words. "It's the way it is. Let it be. Everyone knows about the Road—"

"Holy shit. He like ... like *exploded*. Blood went all over. I'm scared. Please, please tell me what is happening?"

"It's okay. I was shocked the first time I saw it too. You'll come to accept your experience with it. You'll feel better in the morning."

"Feel better..." The woman's voice trailed off.

Dudley glanced at her.

She remained transfixed on whatever the Road Demon showed her. Would it display what she feared, using it as a tool to enter her mind? Would she be able to escape its reign if it did?

"Look away!" Dudley warned.

"No."

"It will use your fear to take your mind."

"It's still hungry."

"What?" Dudley turned to the woman. Her eyes were marble-white, and her pupils had turned the palest blue.

"I'm injured, and it's still hungry," she said, then smiled.

"I-I don't understand."

"Let it be, Dudley Ellington," the woman said in a newfound deep voice. "And don't worry, I'll be seeing you again soon."

She opened her door and jumped out of the moving vehicle.

NEVER SLEEP AGAIN

Though it was against protocol, Reginald Barton sat on the edge of the dresser. If he didn't support his weight, he would collapse. Two drawers lay on the floor, and bloodstained clothes littered the area near his feet. Streaks of sweat ran down his cold cheeks. His stomach rumbled as it hung over his belt.

This is not a dream.

"You okay? You don't look so good." Detective Andrew Washburn ambled over to the dresser when he got no response. "Is it the same?"

Reginald stayed silent, but his gaze drifted toward the bed in the middle of the room, then back to Andrew. His mind churned like a beat-up washing machine. He could hear the heavy *clank*s as he tried to sort through his memories. The morning light made him miserable, especially considering he had only gotten to bed around two a.m. He'd spent the previous night putting an R-and-R soldier-like dent into a bottle of whiskey.

Andrew corrected his pale-yellow tie, which dangled over an ironed blue shirt.

Reginald knew Andrew looked the antithesis of himself with his cropped hazelnut hair, neatly combed; Reginald's own gray hair thinned by the day. Andrew sported a healthy tan; he was pale with patches of pink and was Andrew's senior by thirty years and looked it. Gone were the days Reginald resembled a reputable detective. He appeared more like an ancient janitor now.

Reginald looked back to the bed. The scene made him as miserable as the realizations concerning his own appearance. Two mutilated bodies lay on the floor next to the queen-sized bed; they were Mister and Missus Cable. The first thing that stood out was they had no hands or feet.

"Yeah," Reginald muttered.

"What's that?"

"It's the same."

Silence reigned as both men tried to comprehend the gruesome view. The seconds stretched, and Reginald couldn't resist humming a tune beneath his breath.

"Is this crime inspiring your musical juices?" Andrew asked.

Softly, Reginald sang the same rhyme he had been humming. "Lie safe, lie still, beneath the covers, away from the edge of the bed. Hands and feet safely tucked, or would you rather wake up dead?"

"Well, that's creepy."

"It's loosely translated from an old children's rhyme. Eastern European in origin." Reginald licked his cracked bottom lip. "You never had the fear of something grabbing your hand or foot if it hung over the side of the bed?"

"No."

Reginald headed to the bed. He kneeled, reached under, and swept back some dirt. "See that?" He pointed to the little heap he had made. "It's the same every time. The thing, it's covered in dirt. It always leaves a mess."

"Whoa, easy," Andrew said, raising his hands like a traffic cop telling an oncoming vehicle to stop. "I never said I believed all that. We brought you here so you could confirm any resemblance to all those killings fourteen years ago."

"You read my old reports?"

"Yeah, I scanned over them. Look, Reginald. We believe it's a serial killer. He's been dormant for a while, maybe 'cause you guys put heat on him back then, but we believe he's back. Or it could be a copycat."

"It's no serial killer. I caught—"

"You caught a glimpse of it, or 'one of them' as you put it. Yeah, I read that. Vague description, though."

"It all happened so fast."

"Listen." Andrew stepped toward Reginald and patted his shoulder. "Chief Johnson brought you in. You're retired, and we know how things ended last time. If at any point you want to step away, I'll explain it to Johnson."

Reginald didn't reply. He continued to examine the scene. In his mind's eye, he viewed how the killings may have unfolded.

"I'm going to make a call. Shout if you need me," Andrew said.

Reginald waited for Andrew to leave, then reached into his tattered brown bomber jacket for the little flask sheltered within one of its interior pockets. He took a swig of the vodka, having learned it was less harsh on the breath—not that he cared now.

* * *

A week later, Reginald entered another horrific crime scene. Three people in their early twenties, two males and one female, lay dismembered on the living-room floor. On the coffee table was a half-finished board game, which he couldn't resist investigating.

He stepped back and scanned the scene. "Lie safe, lie still, beneath—"

"Give that a break, will you." Andrew entered from the gray shadows of the kitchen. "Plus, it seems your story has a hole. Their hands and feet are all gone, and there is dirt, but this is the living area—not a bedroom." Andrew walked over to one of the curtains, peeked outside, and returned his gaze to Reginald. "No signs of a break-in."

Reginald pointed.

"What?"

"It's a futon."

"So? Don't tell me that can bend the rules for your monster." Andrew chuckled.

"In a way, it does," Reginald said, heading over to the crimson-stained beige futon with a white-and-blue comforter piled on top. He kneeled, put his hand beneath the futon, and swept back the dirt.

"You have to stop that. We need the forensics to run analysis." Andrew scratched the back of his neck. "Also, I spoke to Johnson. He's upset. Two years from retirement and the maniac you two tried to catch pops up again. I think he wished the killer had already met his mortal end. He doesn't believe it's a copycat. Me? I'm keeping all options on the table."

"Will he be coming around?"

"Nah, he's sick of this shit. To be honest, he doesn't want to see you, even though he recommended bringing you in. Old ghosts, huh?"

"Yeah, something like that."

"So you're still going with...what's that crap, super-na-tural?"

Reginald closed his eyes, sensing a migraine coming.

"We got no fingerprints yet."

"Listen, Andrew. People say I'm washed up, talking shit or something, but will you listen anyway?"

Andrew tapped him on the shoulder. "That's why you're here."

"You see the board game. There are only two pieces in play. The rest are in the box. I counted. None are missing," Reginald said. "One of them, the girl, I believe, was lying on the futon, watching the two guys finish the game. She's key here. She fell asleep. So, maybe one of the guys fetched the comforter for her. Thus my 'monster,' as you put it, was beneath the futon, watching. Once someone is asleep, it comes."

"Damn, I didn't look at the board game."

"Yes, well, I guess it couldn't resist. It watched the two guys playing and drooled over them requiring their hands to move the pieces. They were probably tapping their feet as they laughed and smiled. This must have driven our visitor mad. So it couldn't hold off any longer."

"And all hell broke loose," Andrew finished.

Two forensic examiners dressed head to toe in white suits entered.

"Let's grab a coffee. What do you say?" Andrew asked.

"Sure." The vodka in his pocket wooed Reginald, but caffeine and a few cigarettes would have to suffice for now.

* * *

At the local café, Reginald ordered apple pie as well as a coffee. Andrew had a coffee, black, from which he'd barely taken three sips when he loosened his tie. Reginald sensed Andrew's gaze on him, but he looked at the pie, guessing he was two mouthfuls from its end. Its brown sauce ran down the side of his mouth.

"How is that on the diabetes?" Andrew asked.

"Fuck the diabetes. That's quite the file on me you must have," Reginald said, noticing a ring on Andrew's right hand. Andrew must have received the ring with the red-and-white insignia in college or through his family.

"College football, state champions, in fact."

"Great," Reginald said, annoyed his colleague had caught his gaze.

"Moving on. I must be honest. Last night, I went over some of your old reports."

"Oh yeah? I thought you already scanned them top to bottom." Reginald lifted a scoop of pie.

"You described the thing as having no hands or feet. How could it carry out these gruesome murders?"

Reginald's core knotted. He gazed off into the distance. Andrew, without hard evidence, would never change his opinion from the false idea of a deranged serial killer to what Reginald knew to be true. Turning back to Andrew, he frowned. "We've been over all of this," he said, unable to hold back one last attempt at deflecting the conversation.

"Humor me."

"With its mouth."

"How does it move with no hands or feet?"

"It finds a way."

"And it goes for the extremities? The hands and feet?"

"Yes. After it kills, the hands and feet are the main targets. Also, it was short, four feet, maybe a tad under, real thin, like anorexic. I think—"

"And it wore a white shirt, that it?"

"Yes, a dirty white shirt, far too big for it, hung over its knees. But I was—"

"Man, you get strange people out there," Andrew said, glancing toward one of the servers.

Before Andrew could signal for the bill, Reginald banged the table. "Damn it! You still think this is a man?"

"I'm shooting straight. I told you we believe it's a serial killer. It's possible he uses some trickery, or he's deformed, and obviously, he's disturbed... Nothing more. I'm no longer interested in your theory of a boogeyman or demon manifesting itself under beds, or futons for that matter. I was hoping you might mention the killer having a type of weapon, but no, you've got to say it's a monster severing limbs with its teeth. I can't use that." Andrew exhaled audibly out his mouth. "Your perspective on the scenes, however, can still be beneficial."

Reginald went rigid. His face warmed.

"Reginald. You admitted to it only being a flash. You can't refute it wasn't a man in a getup. As for the height, well, you were scared. Maybe your recollection is fragmented." Andrew lifted the cup of cold coffee, but placed it back down without taking a sip. "You have to end this monster-under-the-bed shit. You're coming off unstable. Things didn't end well the last time. People will talk."

"Oh, and a man simply hides and fits under a bed or futon so easily?"

"Maybe the killer sets the scene to make it look as if he'd been hiding under the bed. Did you ever consider that?"

"Why am I still here? I told you the scenes are the same. Damn it. Get Johnson here if that's all you needed."

"Johnson might not like you, but he still wants you here. I see why. As I said, you're sharp on the scene, but this monster idea is not helping us. We must figure out how this whack job is getting this shit done."

Andrew stood and signaled for the server.

Reginald pushed his wallet deeper in his jacket's pocket. "I must have forgotten my wallet."

"I invited you. I've got this," Andrew said. "I'll call you later. Let me know how a man could do all this, and give me something we can move forward with."

Reginald waited until Andrew left before laboring to his feet, his back creaking as he did. He lit a cigarette, ignoring the frowns around him.

I've tried the rational road. It led me nowhere. If you had seen what I had... The dirty, pale skin, the empty yellow eyes, the stained, razor-sharp teeth, and worse: the disfigured gray stumps this creature had. Oh, and how it moved—it crept, stalked almost. Shit, if you'd seen all this, you'd know better.

* * *

More than two weeks passed before Reginald received another phone call from Andrew. Uneasy concerning what awaited him, he made his way to the home. He entered the bedroom and was knocked back by the stench, having almost forgotten how bad crime scenes could stink.

"We're thinking it's been twenty-four to forty-eight hours. Waiting on the final time-of-death." Andrew handed Reginald a file.

Seventy-three-year-old Caucasian male, it read. Reginald looked at the mutilated body, the severed throat, and the extremities. Only one hand was missing. "That's odd," he said. "Still, the same...case." Reginald had decided to keep his own theories on the identity of the killer to himself. He couldn't extinguish the flame of future vindication, however.

"Yeah, same." Andrew pointed underneath the bed.

Reginald didn't need to kneel to know what was under there. He could already see the dirt lying on the floor.

"Wonder why he only took one hand," Andrew said.

"Yeah, that is weird."

"Well, I'm going to check with the guys in the living room. You can have a look. Shout if you see or figure out anything."

"Will do."

Reginald ambled toward the bed. He stood over the deceased and scanned the room. The only window was open with the curtains drawn closed. The room's yellow light shone, creating the illusion of warmth, but a cool bite circulated the air instead.

He rubbed his hands together, barely able to hear Andrew talking to other officers in the living room. The volume of their voices kept decreasing until they were gone. A crypt-like silence took hold of his world. A low, monotonous ringing began in his ears, and he cupped them and released, trying to clear it. It worked, but the peculiar dull silence returned. He turned to look out the bedroom door. Had Andrew and the other officers stepped outside?

A figure moved in his peripheral vision. Before he could turn, he smelled the pungent stench. It reminded him of the stink of rotten rats left hidden beneath floorboards; the smell was different and more overwhelming than the usual corpse. He could recall only one other time he had experienced such a putrid odor. It was the time he'd seen the creature without hands or feet. He braced against unwelcome shivers as he sought the ominous shape.

There was no doubt it was here.

The creature sat on its legs, on the far side of the bed, staring back at him with crescent-shaped mustard-yellow eyes. It resembled a hairless baboon more than a human. Its gray skin shimmered oddly under the room's light. It had neither feet nor hands—no, Reginald looked again to the right side of the creature. The bloodied thin gray stump that was the creature's arm had a hand impaled on it.

The victim's hand.

Reginald backed away. The creature lifted its right arm and moved it from side to side. The hand rocked unsteadily on the stump, testing the hold. The creature bared its teeth, and a strange idea presented itself in Reginald's mind.

Shit, it's trying to smile and wave at me. It must have seen people do it.

Reginald couldn't believe what he witnessed and stepped back. The creature, seemingly realizing it was getting no reciprocation for its efforts, shuffled forward. Its mood changed. A sinister grin overtook its visage.

The uncomfortable energy in the air was enough to shock Reginald into action. Adrenaline flooded within. He turned around. His large stomach wobbled as he bolted for the door.

After he crossed the threshold into the passage, he banged the door shut. He heard no audible slam.

Holy shit, what the hell?

Streaks of sweat poured down his face, and he gasped for air while searching for calm. Sure, he was out of shape, but the addition of fear made him light-headed. Instinctively, he withdrew the pistol he had concealed in his brown bomber jacket.

Strange sounds pierced the bubble around him.

They became clearer. Someone spoke.

"Reginald, what the hell are you doing?"

It was Andrew.

"Reginald, what's going on? Why do you have a gun?"

"I saw, I... *It.*"

"The man? The killer?" Andrew reached for his sidearm.

Reginald couldn't get any more words out. He stood frigid; tears streaked down his face while his body shuddered.

"Move." Andrew pushed him aside and opened the door, gun at the ready.

Reginald crumpled, sliding down the wall until his rear hit the ground. Other officers entered the room. Muffled voices came, but nothing comprehensible.

As quickly as they had entered, the officers left the room, glancing away from him. Andrew was the last to exit, his gun holstered.

"Pull yourself together, Reginald. There's no one in there."

It took half an hour for Reginald to regain his composure. He was sitting on a blue sofa in the deceased man's living room. How he got there remained hazy. Andrew sat opposite him.

"Your involvement in this is over. Damn it, Reginald. What the hell? If I'd known these murder scenes would push you into a panic attack, I'd never have allowed you on scene," Andrew said, clenching his fists. "You're not cut out for this shit anymore. You know you can't have a gun. The last time you claimed to have seen one of these things, you shot Chief Johnson in the arm. Yes, I know it was an accident, but you panicked then like you panicked today."

Reginald didn't reply. He tried to construct a sentence in his mind, but all sense failed him.

After five minutes of Andrew lecturing him, he finally spoke. "An-drew, I know— I know what I saw."

"Reginald, you stop the bullshit. Do you want to end up in a madhouse? I've spoken to Chief Johnson. We both thank you for your insight."

* * *

A week later, Reginald phoned Andrew.

"Damn it, Reginald. Do you know what time it is? If you don't, let me help you out. It's a quarter past one. My wife is asleep next to me. She'll kill me if I wake her."

"Listen, Andrew," Reginald said. "They're after me. They may come for you as well. They don't want us knowing of them. We got too close."

"Reginald. Please tell me this is not why you're calling me."

"I've noticed dirt under my bed. Not a lot, but it's as though one of them is peeking in. Have you checked under your bed?" Reginald cradled his baseball bat in his lap as he sat on his bed. He wished he still had his gun.

"Reginald, if you don't give this a break, I am going to come over there personally and drag you to the nearest mental asylum. Do you hear me?"

No reply.

"Reginald?"

"I hear you. Be watchful, Andrew."

"Good night."

The line disconnected. Reginald placed down his phone and sat ready to jump if any uninvited visitors arrived. His bedroom light illuminated the room. He gripped the bat tighter as if it were his final tether to the world.

Old eyes grew heavy, and his grip weakened.

* * *

Reginald snorted.

He looked toward the bedroom clock: 2:05 a.m. He'd fallen asleep for nearly an hour, and he cursed himself as he searched the room, a room now draped in darkness—someone had switched off his bedroom light. Managing to make out the light switch on the wall across the room, he took a few heavy steps as the mattress sank in under his weight, and then he leaped toward the switch. He wasn't going to place his leg right next to the bed.

Reginald landed heavily; his old knees pinged with pain, but he blocked it out and stood erect. He switched on the bedroom light and turned around with the baseball bat ready to strike.

The creature sat on his dresser, perched like a gargoyle on a building overseeing the city below. This one had hands and feet impaled on its limbs. It lifted one of *its* hands to wave, then growled.

"Holy shit." Reginald swung the bat.

The peculiar monster moved too slowly, and the bat crashed into its chest. The gray creature left strange splotches of purple liquid behind where it bounced off the wall.

When the creature landed on the floor, Reginald swung again. The hit was a clean blow. Purple liquid splattered everywhere, rebel drops finding Reginald's face. The creature had lost both its feet in its attempt to escape.

It tried to crawl back under the bed.

"Not this time." Reginald brought the bat down on its head.

It stopped moving.

Reginald pushed the creature's lifeless body to the side, wanting to first see if he could figure out how it got around. He placed his bat on the bedside table and lifted his bed, causing his back to crackle. There was nothing but a pile of dirt—no mystery tunnel.

They must be able to open and close portals, or something.

He placed the bed back down and made his way back to the creature.

Now, to figure out what you are.

His gaze locked onto one of the hands still attached to the pale-gray creature, and he ignored the instinct to put both his hands in his pockets. A ring adorned one of the fingers. It had a red-and-white insignia on it.

No, not Andrew.

He marched to the phone and dialed the Washburn residence.

Their phone rang. No one answered.

Reginald looked to the creature. A wave of dizziness washed over him. It was too late to do anything for Andrew, but there was one more call he had to make. Fear and concern dissipated, replaced by the warmth of vindication. He dialed Chief Johnson.

His phone, like Andrew's, rang continuously.

Reginald grunted as he put the handset down.

No, you lazy bastard. You will answer my call. I will be proven right.

He dialed again. This time the phone rang twice before the line went dead.

Useless landlines.

He banged down the handset and cursed. The cell phone his daughter had bought him lay in the living room. An ominous *click* came from his left, and he focused along the wall.

Someone—no, something—had cut the phone wire. It dawned on him that if the creatures had gotten to

Andrew as well as Chief Johnson, their next target was obvious.

Carefully, he made his way toward the passage. His ears were alert and his eyes narrowed as he sought anything off in the room. His bedroom door slammed shut with him only a few steps short of it.

Stumbling backward, he looked to the bed. Dirt was flying out along the sides. He'd gotten the creature that had switched off the lights, but another had bitten the telephone wire and closed him in. It waited for him in the passage. The rest were coming. He searched for his baseball bat and saw it on the bedside table on the other side of the room.

It was too far away.

The blood pumping throughout his body stalled as it froze. Once again, these creatures would keep their existence hidden. Yes, he had been right. Chief Johnson and Detective Washburn had learned this the hard way.

There would be no vindication, however.

42

ANOTHER WARRIOR IN PARADISE

Task One

Seated in a tree overlooking the riverbank, Senghor waited for someone to kill. Ignoring the mosquitoes buzzing around him, he imagined his tribe's secret paradise in his mind's eye, using it as fuel to motivate him for the task. Were the stories of gold huts, copious amounts of food, and endless festivities true? He desired to find out, but he had to carry out three tasks before deserving entry. This was the way of his tribe, and the way it had always been.

Life continuously tested Senghor. Born weak, he had scraped his way into this world. As a youngster, he was skinny and slow; the other kids would often tease him that his parents should've drowned him. A tribe needed strong men and women. He fought against his genetics, only to have to endure his father, Goboka, failing at the ritual three times. It was difficult to look at Goboka now. If Senghor could win, he would restore honor to his family's name.

This was the first year he could take part in the prestigious competition, and he refused to consider failure as the African sun warmed the land, making his breaths long and heavy. The vision of being this year's winner helped ease the humidity's hold on him.

The first task, designed to weed out the weak, would be the hardest. He needed to decapitate another human—and one not from his tribe. He had no special victim in mind. Any other tribe's warrior would do. His focus had been strategy, leading him to the secluded spot. It was unlikely any enemies would hear the screams of their fallen from out here. He could disappear into the jungle if they did.

Crackling came from behind him, and Senghor readied his blade. A figure emerged from the trees to his right. It was a young man with red paintings on his dark body, markings identifying him as a member of a tribe upriver. His slaughter wouldn't find the same admiration as killing an enemy from one of the valleys, but it would suffice.

Under clear cerulean skies, Senghor crept down from the tree. Once his feet hit the earth, he stalked his victim. The young man stretched out his arms as he surveyed the river. He yawned and rubbed his belly. His lack of attentiveness boded well for Senghor.

Senghor stood behind the man, guiding the blade across his victim's throat.

The man turned around, his eyes wide as he flapped his hands over his neck. The blood poured over his fingers. He gurgled as he stepped backward.

Senghor sent the blade into the man's chest.

Crimson drops spurted into the air, but no screams accompanied them.

The man toppled backward, landing hard on the dirt.

Death wasted no time coming for him.

Senghor kneeled and proceeded to cut the fallen man's head off—it took time, but he persevered. As perspiration broke into streams of sweat running down his face, he gazed at the sky. The hour was later than he expected. The afternoon approached. Time was no longer his friend as it had been in the early hours.

With the man's head in his hands, Senghor hurtled through the jungle, trying not to worry that only the first four people who completed the task could move on to attempt the second one. He slowed his pace when he reached the designated spot for the contestants.

"I have done it," Senghor said, dropping the head before him in the clearing surrounded by tall trees.

Kebba, the village chief, nodded and grinned. The movement caused his black-and-gray dreadlocks to bounce around his shoulders. "It seems you are the fourth to complete the task. I wasn't sure if you'd make it." He indicated with his arm to the left.

Three other competitors stood, watching.

Severed heads, all with the white markings of the strongest tribe in the valley, rested at their feet.

"Follow me," Kebba said.

* * *

Task Two

Led to another clearing with a wooden table in its center, Senghor perceived this would be no usual lunch. The pungent reek permeating the area alerted his stomach to trouble. His core rumbled. Yet he persisted, willing himself forward. His competitors shared similar looks of disgust as they hovered around him. What sinister meal would they find underneath the animal skins? He didn't truly want to know, but he hardened his stomach. He had to complete whatever task came.

"Right." Kebba tapped his walking stick on the table. "You will face each other in battles of two. Two winners will go on to the last task. Senghor and Mali will battle first. Take a place before one of the meals."

Mali moved first; Senghor trailed him, ignoring his shaking legs.

At the table he looked at his foe, who was chubby for a warrior. Would that give him an advantage? Senghor ignored the thought, dropping his gaze to the bowl. What was in it? His hopes drifted from unripe fruit to worms. Either would be manageable.

"When I say 'go,'" Kebba said, "you will lift the skin and eat. The one to finish first will be the winner and shall move on."

Mali nodded, but Senghor didn't. He instead pinched his nose with his left hand, as the vile smell coming from below worsened. He steadied his right hand over the skin.

"Go."

Senghor lifted the skin.

A bull testicle, a tail, a snout, intestines, sheep eyes, and other pieces he couldn't identify—and didn't want to identify—were on the menu. People considered a few of the items to be delicacies, but that was when cooked and not rotting, covered with maggots.

He chewed on slug-like blobs first. Green slime spurted from his mouth as he bit into them, and he decided it was best to slurp the rest, swallowing them whole. The stench of decay burned his eyes, causing them to water, but he didn't flinch and grabbed the testicle then shut his eyes. Biting down, he imagined he was in paradise eating fresh grapes and oranges.

When he only had some guts and a few squirming maggots left, he looked to Mali. His competitor was in bad shape. He rocked as if he stood on the deck of a boat in stormy weather, and he had barely eaten anything.

Battling the cramping in his stomach, Senghor finished his unexpected lunch. He lifted the empty bowl and showed it to Kebba.

"Senghor is victorious," Kebba boomed.

Senghor tried to smile, but he failed. He stumbled to the edge of the clearing, hearing Kebba tell the remaining two competitors to get ready. He kneeled behind a tree. The other two competitors had launched into the challenge.

A warm substance shot up his throat like lava, and he opened his mouth wide, vomiting all over colorful flowers next to him. He wiped the perspiration from his brow, trying to inhale through his mouth to avoid the repulsive smell. His body shivered, but he braced himself through the sensation, remembering he had won. He was only one step away from paradise. Thoughts of victory helped against the waves of nausea.

Done retching, Senghor wiped his mouth and looked back.

Abi, the only female competitor, had her arms in the air, victorious. She even smiled and licked her lips. The assortment of revolting snacks hadn't flipped her constitution as it had done to him.

He hadn't expected her to triumph to the final.

The last task was no secret. It stayed the same every year: one of the competitors had to kill the other. It was an event that produced many entertaining stories for campfires. Tomorrow, after he defeated Abi, legend status would be his. He didn't have sympathy for her, as it was an honor to die in battle against the chosen one.

"Abi and Senghor, go now and rest," Kebba said, pointing his stick toward the village. "Tomorrow one of you will fall, while the other will be allowed into paradise."

* * *

Task Three

Morning of the next day brought the battle. By afternoon, one of them would dine in their tribe's hidden nirvana. Energy, like static electricity, coursed through Senghor's veins as he treaded the dirt road to the center of the village. The jungle would hide no more tasks. Now, everyone surrounded him to watch.

He took his place in the circle drawn on the dirt. A warrior of the tribe tossed him a small knife. The muscular man handed one to Abi. The two combatants faced each other.

It was real.

There could be no turning back.

It was a peculiar feeling to look at a woman he'd thought of romantically before, knowing he had to kill and gut her. They had held hands as kids on many occasions and one time by the river she'd kissed him on the cheek. Why had he never made a move for her? He couldn't recall.

Evading the stare of her big brown eyes, he looked to the large wooden bowl alongside him, and then to the one alongside her. They were for the intestines of the fallen competitor. The victor would cut them out before dumping them into a fire, which flamed to Senghor's left. The hypnotic swaying of Abi's hips as she readied herself for combat lured his gaze. Animal skin barely contained her breasts, and she wore different colored beads around her neck.

Kebba walked to the edge of the circle. "Good luck, brave warriors. One of you feasts with the fallen of the tribe tonight in the hereafter, and one of you feasts with the heroes in paradise. There is no shame in either journey, but I know which path I'd prefer."

Kebba banged his stick on the ground.

The fight had begun.

Senghor shot forward. Abi did the same. The crowd clapped and chanted all around him. Not as many called his name as he would have liked, and he ignored the boisterous calls of "Abi, Abi" by lunging for her.

She dodged his first strike.

He came again, kicking at her knee.

She didn't move in time but managed to flick her weapon, slicing Senghor's cheek.

Surprised, he grabbed her leg and lifted her off-balance before plowing her into the earth. He fell on top of her. Luck guided his hand, which plunged his blade between her breasts.

The blood pooled over her chest as she gasped.

The crowd roared in excitement.

To the spectators it must have seemed as if the tackle and stab while falling had been one seamless attack. Senghor was happy to take the acclaim.

He remembered Abi had a knife too and looked to her hands, but there was no threat. The weapon lay on the earth next to her. A quick, merciful death was what he had desired for Abi, and he'd achieved it.

He slit her throat, putting her out of her misery.

The village erupted in applause, whistling, and delirious foot-stomping.

It was not over; he cut underneath Abi's ribs.

After Senghor had tossed Abi's intestines into the fire, Kebba approached. The old chief placed his hand on Senghor's shoulder and said, "The promised land awaits."

* * *

Paradise

The tribe had lined up all along the path to the cave. A palpable silence had infected them as they watched, starry-eyed, while Kebba and other elders led Senghor to the dark entrance. He spotted his mother and father, who both smiled. Yes, he had made them proud and

50

shown that his family was once again worthy of inclusion in the community. It was now time for his reward.

"You know what to do?" Kebba asked.

Senghor nodded.

He'd studied proceedings last year, when the brave warrior Moku had earned entry to his tribe's heaven on earth. It was time for him to unburden himself from the trappings of the normal. There would be only the best robes and clothing inside. He stripped and dropped his clothes along with his knife to the earth.

Naked, he listened as one of the elders chanted a song.

A few of the villagers hummed along.

What awaited him inside? The excitement made his stomach tingle like the time he had eaten an unripe mango when he was a child. Rumors did the rounds that the cave was only a path, and that it led to a hidden valley of wonder. Here, the former warriors lived their days in bliss. It was a stretch to also believe the tale that angels served the fallen warriors, but Senghor wouldn't complain if it were true.

"It is time." Kebba pushed Senghor forward. "Senghor, you have done our village proud. Your name will echo around these lands for eternity like the great ones before you. Go now, great warrior Senghor."

Senghor entered.

The people outside returned to their initial silent state.

Deeper into the dark cave Senghor ventured. He was worried the blackness would swallow him, but rebellious beams of light shone down from above every few steps. It was enough for him to see his way forward. Stones shifted underfoot, but he endured as a mixture of fear and excitement danced within his stomach like bees around a hive.

The passageway gradually appeared to slope downward, and he had to relax his pace, even if all he wanted was to run.

He craved paradise.

Time felt like an illusion in the shadowy world. He stretched his arms, feeling the rough, rocky walls on both sides. His path had become narrower, which was unexpected, but, before panic could claim dominion over his mind, beams of light rained over him.

He entered a large chamber, illuminated brighter than anywhere else on his journey so far. The downpour of light gave the cavern the appearance of dusk. Paradise *must* be nearby. Senghor had to calm himself at the realization. He glanced around. Did another passageway lead to his desired destination?

Stone walls greeted him in every direction.

Something cracked under his right foot. It was a white object, now broken in half. He picked it up.

It was a bone—human.

"This is not right," he muttered.

A strange sensation tickled his skin, as if drizzle hit him. He knew this couldn't be and looked up. White strings falling from above glimmered when rays of light hit them. He held out his arms and saw the strands over them. Trying to wipe them off, he found they were sticky and unwilling to leave his limbs.

"What is this?" He stepped forward, but his left foot wouldn't budge. It had become tangled in the white substance.

He wore no clothes to protect himself.

He had no knife to cut himself free.

Noise from above caused him to lift his gaze. A brown eight-legged arachnid, which he guessed was five or six feet in length, descended from the cavern ceiling, like a leaf in the breeze. This couldn't be real. Was he poisoned at some point? This had to be a hallucination. No, he'd heard whispers of this beast around campfires.

J'ba Fofi—the legend of the giant spider was true.

It crawled toward him, slowly at first, but it must have sensed he was well and truly stuck, as it then jumped forward.

Fangs pierced his flesh. Heat and pain infiltrated his body, first at the point of the bite, but then it spread everywhere. His hands curled like claws as a poison claimed control over his limbs. He couldn't scream. His jaw had locked shut.

The pain turned to numbness, and unable to move, his body tipped backward.

He dropped to the floor covered in the bones of other warriors.

The years of training, the tasks, and even the last battle were not for the tribe to figure out who was worthy of the land of bliss and glory. They were to decide one worthy of *sacrifice*. Was this what kept the J'ba Fofi appeased in its cave? Senghor recalled other tribes also had rituals similar to his own. How long had these sacrifices been going on? He didn't know, but one fact hardened like rock in his mind.

Paradise was a lie.

HER HEART BEATS FOR ANCIENT BEASTS

The young man, aged between twenty-one and twenty-five, burst out from a line of trees clutching at his throat. Blood spurted from his neck, changing a once-white T-shirt to red. The man gurgled and grunted as his pace slowed to a zombie-like shuffle. He extended his right arm as he fell forward and landed on the hard soil underfoot. It appeared he had no more energy to crawl the last few feet he needed to reach the dirt road.

"Shit," Officer Rupert Stone said as he hurried to the man. He called in for an ambulance, but all he got back was static. "Hey, man. Are you okay? What the fuck happened?"

The man didn't move; Officer Rupert checked his vitals, hoping the injuries weren't as serious as they looked. "Come on, dude."

The man showed no signs of life.

Officer Rupert stood, bracing through the unease that rattled his nerves, then kicked at the dusty ground beneath his feet. The action did little to alleviate his growing shock and anger. He breathed in deep, trying to ignore the spicy, earthy aroma of his current location.

He loathed the wild in general, but he especially despised this part of town. The southern outskirts were for the hippies, the homeless, and the bugs. Why did he have to stop by Lucinda during work hours? Had he not, he wouldn't have been close enough to the area to receive the call from dispatch. If only she had taken his advice and moved into town.

A branch breaking alerted him to movement on his right. He turned, surveying the line of trees, while instinctively going for his firearm.

"Well, shoot me in the leg and call me Hop-Step Stevie," Duncan Kittle said as he walked toward Officer Rupert. "Miracles do still happen."

"What?" Officer Rupert asked.

Duncan had a large, round belly and balding gray hair. He wore a white "Welcome to Idaho" T-shirt that was at least two sizes too small, particularly around his midsection. Duncan owned substantial amounts of land in this part of town. Realtors had deemed these purchases as clever investments at one point, but it was no longer the case with their once-prosperous small town following the fate of the forgotten before it.

"I've called multiple times over the last few years. You're the first cop to come out. These damn trespassers. I usually ignore them, but now I've had it and decided to scare them off myself. What the fuck happened to him?"

"He's dead. Isn't he who you called about?"

"No." Duncan frowned as he surveyed the deceased. "I called about some damn woman that was screaming like a mad thing all morning."

"Drop the weapon," Officer Rupert said, realizing Duncan was holding a hunting rifle.

"What? You think I did this? The man wasn't shot, you fool." He pointed at the man's chest. "Check out the gash in his chest. Plus, his throat's been cut."

Officer Rupert looked over the body, shifting his hand away from his firearm as he realized Duncan was correct. "Well, I wonder what went down here. Do you know anything?"

When Officer Rupert had arrived, he'd parked his vehicle alongside the main road, then searched around for who'd reported the incident to dispatch. When nobody appeared, he had ventured along the dirt side road on foot, unsure exactly where it led. There was a trailer park farther up the main road, followed by a ramshackle barn, a dried-up dam, a few homes—including Lucinda's—then a gas station with a rickety old sign, but what awaited him on the current path, he couldn't recall. He hadn't expected he would be walking toward a murder scene.

"Hey," Officer Rupert said, "I asked what the hell happened here?"

"Shit. Wild animal or wild human? I don't know. Maybe the woman I heard screaming would know more."

Officer Rupert needed to get back to his vehicle to inform the station about what had happened. He also wanted to find this woman, especially if she was involved in the murder. If she got away, he would be responsible. How hard could it be to catch a crazy woman, anyway? "Where do you think she is?"

"The caves."

* * *

There were two paths to the caves. Officer Rupert traversed one and Duncan walked the other. If they found the woman, they would apprehend her and call the other to their location.

As the flora around him grew wilder and the path narrowed, Officer Rupert remembered that the caves were located in a few of the rocky hills in the area, probably homes to some of the town's outcasts. He shook his head, bracing through the thought of encountering vagrants reeking of trash and other putrid odors. It didn't matter who he came across, though—he would detain all of them until he had answers about the murder. He smiled, realizing this was an opportunity to show his value to the force and the community. After his transfer here five months ago, following a failed marriage in a neighbouring town, this could truly kick-start the new beginning he desired.

The path led him down a slope, which opened to a little valley surrounded by small hills. The caves were easy to spot. They were unimpressive, and were relegated to the hill on his right, thus calling all his focus. He considered drawing his firearm but dismissed the idea, not wanting to rattle a potentially unhinged suspect unnecessarily.

"Is anyone here?" he asked the world around him.

Silence.

He placed his hands on his hips and surveyed the area, seeking anything that might be off. Even though there was no noise, he had a sense of being watched. Wasn't that always the feeling in these situations?

"Is anyone here?"

Still no reply came, and he strolled toward the nearest cave. What was keeping Duncan? The man knew the area better than him. What if he had come across the woman? Just as Officer Rupert turned to go assist him, a shape in the cave caught his eye.

He marched into the shadow the cave provided, but his legs wobbled with every step as he realized what lay in the cave: a body.

It was Lucinda.

How? He had been with her earlier that day when she'd radiated so much life. Now, her neck had been slashed and other gashes and cuts covered her body. Blood drenched her favorite blue dress and had mixed into the dirt all over the cave's floor. Officer Rupert knelt next to her, checking for a pulse or any sign of breathing.

Lucinda was dead.

* * *

Upon exiting the cave, Officer Rupert stood almost spellbound. It felt as if minutes were passing by, but he knew it was only seconds. Perspiration ran free down his arms, and his pulse thundered in his head. He resisted the urge to cry and then to punch anything and everything around him. What was going on? What the fuck was going on? He needed to remain composed and professional, to get back to his vehicle as fast as he could, and then notify dispatch. The feeling of being watched returned, except it was more intense than earlier, as if true evil had entered this realm.

"What are you doing?"

Officer Rupert turned to his left, drawing his firearm as he did. The voice was that of a young woman, but for some reason he expected to see the Devil.

She approached him, draped in a dirty white dress; her brown boots almost left no marks in the earth in her wake. Her platinum-blonde hair hung wild, clearly in need of a wash. Even with her disheveled appearance, her eyes remained resplendent and pierced the distance between them. What emotion were they conveying? Was it concern? Was it fear? Was it guilt? It was hard to read her.

"Stop right there," Officer Rupert said, aiming the gun at her.

"We don't have time for this. It will be back."

"What are you talking about?"

She pointed to the cave behind him. "The thing that killed the woman. It will return and we need to hide."

"Is it an animal?" Officer Rupert asked. The question brought traces of hope that an animal could be behind these heinous crimes as opposed to a fellow human. The wounds of both victims seemed calculated and identical, however, pointing away from the wild attack of an animal. What animal could it even be? He racked his brain trying to think of a species, other than his own, that could be so cold and calculated when killing, but also one that could inhabit this area. Nothing came to the fore of his mind. "Are you saying it's an animal?"

The woman shrugged. "Kind of."

"What do you mean?"

"It resembles nothing you've seen or known of. Its shape appears unnatural, as if it disobeys understood proportions. It isn't covered in fur, feathers, scales, or skin. Instead, a shimmering kaleidoscope of colors teases where its surface might be. It moves fast and slow at the same time. It's older than man and has roamed—"

"What the hell are you talking about? I don't have time for this. I'm placing you under arrest. Turn around and—"

The woman turned around as instructed, but then sprinted into the woods.

"Shit," Officer Rupert said, running after her.

* * *

They headed deeper and deeper into the woods. Sticks broke underfoot. Branches scratched at his body. His desire to apprehend the woman had overcome his fear of entering the wild initially, but as the pursuit continued, he couldn't shake the dread of finding trouble. It was possible, after all, that something or someone other than the woman had committed the murders.

Voices could be heard up ahead. He increased his pace while trying to be mindful of his surroundings. Someone was shouting.

He entered a clearing, only to see the woman standing still. Ahead of her Duncan stood with his rifle aimed at her.

"Please," the woman said, "we need to get away from here before it returns. I can help you."

"Help me? You tried to kill me." Duncan scoffed and pointed to a cut on his face. "Hit me with a damn rock. You could've blinded me."

"I'm sorry. I thought you were going to hurt me."

"I own this land and now you want to tell—"

"Be quiet and listen." The woman placed her index finger over her mouth. "Don't you hear it out there?"

"I don't hear anything."

Officer Rupert endeavored to listen intently, still speculating if there was something else out there. He heard nothing, which in itself was strange. Where was the buzzing of insects, the crackling of branches, or the rustling of leaves? It was as if they had stepped into another realm. Still, he didn't hear anything to suggest that there was a monster approaching. There, the woman was incorrect.

"Don't you feel its presence?" she asked Duncan.

"No."

Officer Rupert did feel another presence. Ever since he had arrived, he'd felt as if he was being observed by something, something ominous that lurked in the shadows. He could've blamed it on the woman, except here she was, and he still had the peculiar sensation.

"I'm sorry, but I've got to go," the woman said.

"No chance." Duncan looked to Officer Rupert. "Arrest her."

There was a strange conflict within Officer Rupert. The woman had to be apprehended and hit with the full capabilities of the law if she'd murdered Lucinda and the other man, but he also desired for her to continue talking about the presence that she believed haunted this area. Maybe he could slip in a few of his own questions after he detained her?

The woman picked up a rock.

"Don't," Duncan said.

She hurled it at him, missing his head by a few inches. Duncan, however, fired his rifle. The bullet hit the earth less than a yard to the woman's right. She turned and darted toward the woods. Duncan aimed again.

"Don't do it," Officer Rupert said, pointing his handgun at Duncan. "I will go after her and arrest her."

"This is my land. She tried to kill me." Duncan fired.

Officer Rupert fired, too.

Duncan's bullet vanished into the woods. Officer Rupert's bullet went through Duncan's chest.

Duncan toppled to his knees, whining in pain. He dropped his rifle and tried to lift his shirt, but his shaking arms failed him.

"Ah...shit," Officer Rupert said. "What have I done?" He made his way toward Duncan, just as the man collapsed forward onto the ground. "I told you not to fire, you idiot." He turned Duncan onto his back. Should he try dragging Duncan to his vehicle, or should he run to his vehicle and get dispatch to send help? How much time did Duncan have?

"We have to get him to the cave," the woman said, emerging from the tall trees to Officer Rupert's left.

"What? I need to get him help."

"We need to complete the ritual. There isn't much time left in this cycle. Do you want to join him?"

"What are you on about?" Officer Rupert stood and marched to the woman. He grabbed her dress and tugged so hard she had to correct her balance. "I'm tired of this bullshit. You tell me exactly what is going on here, now."

"I know you feel it. Help me get his body to the caves and I will explain everything to you."

"I—I don't want— Listen, you will do as I say."

"No."

Officer Rupert grabbed his handcuffs. The woman reached for an item as well, and by the time he realized what it was, the bloodied blade had exited his abdomen.

"You...stabbed me," he said, shuffling backward.

"I'm sorry. You didn't listen."

How bad was the wound? Officer Rupert didn't dare look. He tried to apply pressure as he stepped farther back from the woman. Would she attack him again? He considered reaching for his weapon, but she hadn't moved since attacking him. The world around him blurred; he was about to faint.

* * *

Officer Rupert drifted in and out of consciousness. As he struggled to determine his situation, he understood he was being dragged. Was it the woman or did she have an accomplice? Maybe it was her monster, taking him off to be devoured? That was nonsense, of course. It was more likely the woman had rolled his body onto something easier to drag to her desired destination.

That did open other questions. Where was she taking him? The caves were quite a distance away. Surely, she didn't have the energy to transport both him and Duncan there. How much time had passed since he shot Duncan? Was Duncan still alive? What was she going to do with him?

His eyes grew heavy.

He faded out.

* * *

Officer Rupert opened his eyes again. Wheezing from his chest and sharp pains in his gut alerted him to the fact that he hadn't passed on yet, while dizziness rocked him as he raised his neck to ascertain his surroundings and current predicament.

The woman knelt at the cave's entrance. "I thought you might be different, but you're a stubborn nonbeliever. Maybe if we had more time, you would've seen and felt the truth."

"You're nuts," Officer Rupert muttered. His mouth tasted like copper. "You need help, serious help."

"Soon the ritual will be complete, and our town will continue for another cycle."

Pain shot like a bolt through Officer Rupert's abdomen. If he didn't get help soon, he would bleed to death. He couldn't believe he was going to go out thanks to a nutjob who believed in some ancient beast. If he hadn't gone to Lucinda, he wouldn't have been near enough to take the call. He should've waited until the weekend to see her. Then they both would've carried on with their lives, oblivious to this bullshit.

"Why did you kill Lucinda?" he asked.

"Who?"

"The woman in the other cave, with the blue dress."

"Oh, her. I tried to help her. She saw your vehicle as she headed into town and stopped to see what was going on. I told her to stay away, but she didn't listen. She knew where the caves were and was concerned for you. Luckily, she didn't take the same path as you."

"Who helped you? How many people have you killed?"

"Quiet now. They're almost here." The woman stood, then wiped her knees.

"Who is almost here?"

The woman ignored him.

Four figures arrived at the entrance of the cave alongside the woman. Don Cornell, the town's mayor, stood to the far left. Next to him was Brad Oakley, an entrepreneur and popular real estate agent. Next to Brad stood Kimberly Watkins, a local business magnate. The last of the four was Pat Barker, the town's police chief. All of them sported the same solemn look.

"I wrapped the wound to slow his bleeding," the woman said. "I think he does have internal damage. You'll need to decide fast."

Decide what? Officer Rupert struggled to process what was going on. Why hadn't the police chief arrested the woman at once? Why didn't they get him help?

Mayor Cornell held his arm out, then made a thumbs down.

Brad Oakley did the same.

Kimberly Watkins followed suit.

The three of them turned around and walked away, never recognizing Officer Rupert or even glancing his way.

"I'm sorry, Rupert," Police Chief Barker said, dropping his gaze. "I thought you had promise. I hoped for something different for you, but majority rules."

"What? What are you fucking on about?" Officer Rupert shouted through burning lungs. "Get me help, you son of a bitch."

Police Chief Barker ignored him and turned to the woman. "How many do you still require for the ritual?"

"Including him, there are eight. So one more."

"Okay." Police Chief Barker nodded. "Officer Martinez picked up some drunk homeless guy near the bar this morning. I'll have him brought around to you."

"Thank you."

Police Chief Barker walked away.

"Wait, you bastard!" Officer Rupert shouted.

It was to no avail. None of them returned. Officer Rupert tried to move, hoping he could find adrenaline to crawl, but his attempts were forlorn, as every movement rocked his rib cage with intense pain, making it hard to breathe.

"Help me." His voice was barely audible.

The woman walked away.

The feeling of being watched resurfaced.

THE RIVER RAN RED

The river ran red. It wasn't the first time Asani had seen the peculiar occurrence, but it transfixed him all the same. He had once gone upstream in search of what caused the crimson color. Angry voices and the pounding of spears on shields had stopped him from quenching his curiosity.

Not this time.

He moved between the branches of the trees along the river, inhaling the plethora of aromas from citrus-sweet to damp and musky. The humidity of the Western African atmosphere caused salty perspiration to run down his face. It didn't bug him anymore. This was his real home, and he loved the jungle.

His mother had taken him away from here after his father's passing. The village they had relocated to bored him. There was even a school now, and his mother had forced him to attend from the first day it opened. It wasn't for him. Asani longed for the old ways. The stories his uncle had told him captivated him. He wanted to be like the village's warriors. He wanted to learn the old methods of doing things, as well as to hunt animals, and fight enemy tribes—the last wish was really a dream because such violence had stopped many years before. Getting to visit his uncle, who stayed in a village in the jungle, a village that still had some resemblance of their ancestor's ways, was heaven.

A harrowing scream caused him to pause.

Asani's intestines knotted. It was a male, but the man was either so scared or in so much pain that he didn't sound too far from being a pig when slaughtered. There were many different predators within the jungle, and many of them could do a man harm. Asani reached toward his hip and retrieved the knife he had brought with. The handle was rough, and a splinter pricked his thumb as he tightened his grip. Rays of sunlight piercing the canopy of branches overhead reflected off the blade, shining on the trunk of a nearby tree.

There was a handprint on the trunk.

It shared the crimson color of the river.

Something disturbed the bush to his side. A branch snapped. Asani didn't see anything moving and kept low, making his way toward the sound. If it was an animal, and he caught it, he would gain some much-needed respect. Putting the man's scream to the back of his mind, he inhaled deeply. "Straight for the throat" was the advice he'd received when asking about how the tribe had become such proficient hunters and killers.

He came out from a bush covering him, stumbling across an open path.

The path was man-made, created by his village, and Asani looked ahead, wondering where it led.

Figures appeared on the path. Asani's heart shuddered, and his mind commanded him to take flight. It was too late. His uncle had seen him; his uncle saw everything. The seconds that passed as the men approached him were insufferable. Asani feared his uncle would send him straight home, or worse, scold him in front of the group.

His uncle did neither.

He waited for the rest of the men with him to walk ahead. None bothered to look at Asani, as if he didn't exist.

With no witnesses in sight, his uncle placed a hand on his shoulder and gripped down hard. "What are you doing here?"

Asani needed a satisfactory answer and fast. His uncle's eyes burned his own. "I was hunting."

"So far from the village?"

"I didn't realize I'd wandered so far."

His uncle frowned. "Did you hear or see anything?"

Asani wasn't sure if his uncle meant animals or something else. Was it a test? He tried to remain calm, hoping no tells surfaced. The man's scream echoed in the fore of his mind, but he hastily searched for another thought, one of a jungle, chirping and buzzing.

"No," Asani said.

* * *

The following morning, a gentle breeze danced around the village. Asani stepped out of his uncle's hut, knowing that the cool atmosphere wouldn't last long. He walked past one of the elder women, who tended a fire she had made.

"You hungry?" she asked, stirring the black pot that hung over the flames.

Asani shook his head.

He wanted to return to the river and find out what had happened to the man there the previous day, but he couldn't see his uncle anywhere and was afraid of running into him again. The aroma of porridge and fresh bread flooded his sense of smell. Maybe something to eat wasn't a bad idea while he contemplated a course of action. There would be daily chores lined up for him, but they were the furthest things from his mind.

He turned back to the woman, but she had left with her pot.

Asani took a seat by what remained of the fire, hoping she would return. The sensation of a centipede crawling over his back tickled, and he looked around the village, searching for anything out of the ordinary. All he saw were the villagers doing their chores: women preparing breakfast or washing animal furs, men sharpening spears or adding wood to various fires, and kids running around.

Yet something wasn't right.

The sounds of hundreds of birds taking flight emanated from the trees on the perimeter of the village. They ascended into the pellucid sky. Then came screaming, much like the man Asani had heard the day before. He looked ahead. A man rushed out from the line of trees, wearing nothing but some animal fur over his lower half.

Blood covered the man's face.

Asani stepped to his right, sensing the man would run straight into him. Instead, he turned and ran away from the village, screaming and thrashing his arms about as if something were eating him alive.

Villagers moved out of his path.

Asani stood in a trance. The man vanished from his view. No one in the village paid any attention to him, apart from getting out of his way. Once the man was gone, they carried on with whatever tasks they had been doing.

It didn't add up.

"Psst... Over here."

Searching for the voice, Asani looked at one of the girls from the village. She indicated for him to follow her as she ducked between two huts. It hadn't been the first time he'd noticed her. It had, however, been the first time she'd spoken to him. She was by far the most attractive girl he had seen in the village with her toned, slender limbs and long black hair. Her eyes softened as she gestured again with her hand for him to follow her into the jungle.

Asani obeyed.

They walked for about twenty minutes before her pace slowed, and she stopped abruptly, turning to him.

She placed her index finger over her lips. "Shhh."

Asani didn't hear anything but obeyed.

"Okay." She stepped toward him. "I saw you were surprised by the man running through the village. I'll tell you about him. But first, I'm going to show you the circle of madness. Have you seen it before?"

Asani shook his head.

"Good. I'm Fahimah. I've seen you around. You come and go. Your uncle is the leader of our tribe. You must be special?"

Warmth rose from the base of Asani's neck. "I-I'm Asani. I usually stay in another village with my mother. I visit here every now and again."

Fahimah nodded, indicating for him to follow again. She stalked her way past low-growing bushes and tall trees with narrow trunks. The normal sounds of the jungle had disappeared, making the silence an unusual event.

They entered a clearing where the sun warmed Asani's face. He looked around. Oval-shaped rocks formed a circular perimeter around them.

"That man you saw running through the village was not cured." Fahimah pointed at one of the rocks. "Do you see the drawings?"

Asani walked to the rock. Someone had painted a creature on its smooth gray surface. It was unlike any animal he had seen with saber-like canines, scales over its body, and a long tail. Its most intimidating feature was the horn on its head. Around the monster, severed human limbs floated.

"What is it? What is this place?" Asani asked, looking to the rock on his right, where he saw a river painted red.

"That is the Dingonek, or as some people call it, the Jungle Walrus. It lives somewhere in the river far from the village. This place, as I told you, is the circle of madness. It is where some warriors come if they have side effects from the ritual. They draw on the rocks, scream, and do other things until the evil and madness have left them."

Asani remembered the crimson section of the river and the man who screamed. Surely this was all just a tale. A creature in the river? A ritual? The tribe had stopped a lot of the old ways. Hadn't they?

"You don't know about the ritual?" Fahimah asked, walking toward him.

Asani shook his head. "No. I also find this monster hard to believe."

"I can't speak confidently about the Dingonek—I've only heard the tales. But the ritual? That's very real. It's going on this very week. The man you saw running through the village must have failed. Not even the circle of madness will be able to cure him, I think. He'll never become an elder in the tribe now. Might even be sent away...if he ever returns."

Asani strode to another of the rocks. This one had a man holding a skull high into the air.

"Why is the skull red?"

"Some say it's because the water stains it after a while, others say it's because of the evil of the creature, and some say it's from all the blood spent in the river. The ritual is not always passed."

"What is the rit—"

Fahimah pulled him down to the ground, hard, before he could speak further. She held her hand over his mouth. The skin on her fingers was soft, yet her grip firm.

"Quiet," she said, "someone is coming. We must go. Follow me."

Asani crawled behind Fahimah until they reached the safety of the jungle. They then hid behind some bushes, waiting to see who came.

His uncle and other men appeared.

They huddled in the clearing, near the circle of rocks, but no one entered the circle as he and Fahimah had. Asani could hear them talking. It was hard to understand exactly what they said due to the distance and the return of the jungle's sounds.

"...tomorrow...he will do us proud..." someone said.

"...today was bad...barely got in..."

"...he didn't die..."

"...death might have been better..."

One voice was clearer than the rest. Asani's uncle said, "I have no doubt tomorrow will be a good day. Tumo's son is brave. He is a fighter. He will pass the ritual."

* * *

Asani woke up in darkness. He'd willed his mind the night before not to let him oversleep, and it had listened. It didn't take long for the early morning to illuminate the dark hut. His uncle got up and fumbled with something in the shadows.

Asani tried to watch his uncle under almost shut eyes.

His uncle reached for his spear and then attached a knife to a band around his waist. Beneath his breath, he prayed, kneeling in the pale light.

The ritual ruled Asani's thoughts. What was it? Could he pass it? Would they allow him to attempt it? Would he gain the tribe's respect then? He sometimes sensed how they looked at him and what they thought. Coming from more modern ways, he didn't doubt they thought him weaker, maybe even unworthy of the tribe.

He had told Fahimah he'd join her later that day. She was beautiful and intriguing; he enjoyed the moments he spent with her, but she was no match for the glory of having the entire tribe's respect. He just needed to know what the ritual entailed.

His uncle grabbed his shield and exited the hut.

Asani slunk out behind him, carefully, so as not to draw attention.

His uncle moved fast and splashed his face in a large bowl of water, before accepting some porridge and something to drink from one of the women seated at a fire. Clearly not wanting to waste time, his uncle downed the drink and finished breakfast with large, fast gulps.

Asani's stomach groaned as he followed behind his uncle. He ducked behind a hut, sensing his uncle might look back.

A group of men, also armed with spears and shields, joined up with his uncle, including a younger-looking man whom his uncle patted on the back. The warriors around him obscured the man's face.

The group then headed into the jungle.

Asani followed, reaching down for his knife. He felt nothing but air where the weapon should be.

There wasn't time to fetch it from the hut.

He wandered into the jungle, where a mystical quality mesmerized in the early hours. The sun hadn't heated the world to unbearable temperatures yet, and shadows created the illusion of secret realms hidden from the usual world. The earthy smell was strong, but so, too, were the other spicy and sweet aromas of the natural world. Every unexpected sound could potentially be a wild animal. It was a world where anything could happen.

Things changed when the men continued on the narrow path Asani had discovered yesterday. Now, he had to keep well back from his uncle and the other men. There were no trees or bushes to hide behind, any mistake would give him away. Sometimes, he had to hold back until he could just make out their voices. Fortunately for him, the men had begun singing once out of earshot of the village.

They disappeared ahead, taking a left off the path.

Asani pursued them, cringing every time he stumbled on the uneven ground, as each ill step or shuffle caused the earth to moan, whether it be leaves rustling or branches snapping underfoot. Eventually, he was near enough to observe where the men had gone.

They stood around a part of the river that had almost formed a circle. This area of the river was surrounded by tall trees with hanging branches. It was a peculiar sight. Asani had become so accustomed to the narrow snake-shaped river that the new spot came across like a little paradise hidden away in the jungle. He imagined how blissful it would be to swim here.

His uncle and the other men aimed their spears at the water's surface. Their shields were in place, protecting their bodies. Asani ignored the wobble in his knees. The younger man, Mwamba, Asani believed his name was, had not done as the rest. Mwamba stood, praying.

"Mwamba, are you ready? Are you ready to be an elder and pass this ritual?" Asani's uncle asked. "You only have to retrieve one skull, and you're one of us. We've all done it before. We know you can do it."

Mwamba nodded.

"It's morning. The Dingonek sleeps. He only wakes in the evening. Do not be afraid, Mwamba, son of Tumo. Are you ready?"

Mwamba nodded.

"I said are you ready?"

"Yes," Mwamba muttered.

"Go now."

Mwamba dived into the river.

Asani wanted to laugh at the silly myth created as part of the ritual. This couldn't be easier. The images on the rocks had reminded him of the drawings of kids in his school, and he wondered if the circle of madness was also an invention to add to the mystique of the ritual. The monster meant to inhabit the river was the most ridiculous of all.

Mwamba splashed around, forceful, not the sound one would associate with normal swimming.

Asani stood, stealthily, trying to see what had caused the man's actions.

"Just relax. Get the skull," his uncle said to Mwamba.

Mwamba ducked below the surface.

When he came up again, he wasted no time swimming back to shore, where he fell to his knees and raised the reddened skull above his head. Asani's uncle and the rest of the men patted him on the back, whispering congratulations.

"Let's go," his uncle said. "The Dingonek will be upset at someone disturbing the balance of death in the river. We will celebrate properly back in the village."

Asani had seen and heard enough.

He crept out from his hiding spot. "Uncle, I wish to perform the ritual next."

His uncle's eyes widened, his mouth opened, and Asani realized it was a look of shock—a look he had never seen on his uncle's face. His uncle became reanimated and indicated for the rest of the men to leave them.

"What are you doing here?" he asked Asani once they were alone.

"I want to do the ritual."

"That's not how it works. Only those invited may attempt it. All the men have now seen you here, breaking our ways. You're a real embarrassment, Asani. This is sacred."

"That's stupid." Asani stomped his foot. "It's so silly I could pass it in my sleep."

His uncle pushed him in the chest, hard, sending Asani reeling backward until he lost balance and fell onto his rear. Tears built up in his eyes. The denial of the chance to do the ritual and then the physical contact brought feelings of anger and shame to the surface.

"I can do it, Uncle," Asani muttered. "And then the village will respect me."

"No."

His uncle reached down, grabbed Asani's arm, and yanked him up.

"We're leaving this place. You are never to come here again. Do you understand, Asani?"

Fearing more punishment, Asani nodded.

A tear streaked down his cheek.

* * *

The afternoon heat was particularly unforgiving. Asani didn't mind. It reflected his inner turmoil. The anger, humiliation, and pain feasted like maggots inside of him. The first of his punishments was to help clean some of the pots used during lunch. This would have tipped him over the edge had another fire not burned within his mind once he'd arrived back in the village. He was biding his time, waiting for the opportunity to head into the jungle.

Nothing would stop him performing the tribe's silly ritual.

He'd retrieve one of the red skulls, and everyone would respect him.

When some of the elder people began heading into their huts, to take naps before the evening's festivities in honor of Mwamba, Asani dropped what he was doing. He retrieved his knife and headed into the jungle, watchful for prying eyes.

He didn't know the exact route, but he knew that if he followed the river upstream, he could check for the path that led to the ritual's special place. Feeling better than he had all day, he couldn't help but chuckle. He imagined the villagers' faces of shock and awe when he returned with the skull. He didn't wish to spoil the festivities for Mwamba, who seemed nice, but the village and his uncle had brought it upon themselves. They would respect him and celebrate him as well. Maybe he could even convince his mother that this was the place for him.

He would be an esteemed elder after all.

Maybe one day he could even replace his uncle as the tribe's leader.

Asani's cheeks felt sore, and he noticed he was grinning. Pausing to look around, he decided to move away from the river, hopeful he would come across the path.

He did.

It was all so easy, as if the gods had already written his destiny in stone. Ignoring the usual precautions of being in the jungle, Asani started jogging up the path. He wanted it all, now.

When he came across the river, he didn't wait.

Asani dived right in.

The water was not only warmer than he expected, but it was also clearer. He glanced down, then lowered his head into the water, wondering where he would find one of the skulls. As he scanned the rocky riverbed, it occurred to him he might not find one. Maybe they were placed here before the ritual?

He cursed himself as he raised his head above the surface.

Biting his tongue, he decided it best to look around before conceding defeat. It remained possible a skull had been forgotten. He submerged himself again, seeking an area to inspect before kicking himself to the bottom, where he swam, searching the rocks on the riverbed for anything that stood out.

It didn't take long for him to notice red become the dominant shade in the river. Looking ahead, Asani realized he would have no problem finding a skull. There were many. Along with the skulls, there were other bones dyed with red, most of them shattered. He needed to breathe, but the urge to grab one of the skulls was stronger.

He stuck his fingers into the eye sockets of the nearest skull and headed back to the surface, now wondering why there were so many—at least twenty to thirty of them were visible. He could understand why the village would want to make it easy for the challengers doing the ritual, which really was just an elaborate ruse to scare the men and test their bravery, but where would they find so many skulls and why were other bones scattered over the river's floor as well? Were they animals?

Surfacing, he looked at the skull in his hand.

It was human.

When the river was shallow enough for him to walk, he decided not to worry about the amount of human bones in the river. Maybe the tribe had some strange ritual after all, like instead of burying their dead, they dropped them into the river. Whatever the reasoning behind the bones, it didn't matter. He had retrieved one of the skulls. He would gain their respect and become one of the elders.

Asani got down on one knee and raised the skull when he stepped on land, mimicking Mwamba. No one patted his shoulder or congratulated him, but he imagined them doing so.

As he stood again, heat, like someone starting a fire, erupted over the back of his right leg.

Something white and sharp protruded through his right thigh.

Asani looked at the object in disbelief. His world wobbled like the time he had drunk alcohol for the first time. He touched the object, which now looked like an animal horn, and as he did, pain exploded from the wound throughout his body.

The horn disappeared, leaving a hole in the middle of his leg.

Asani braced himself by widening his stance and trying to find equilibrium as his body swayed like a small tree hit by intense winds. He heard splashing as he turned back to the river.

Asani stared upon the Dingonek.

The drawing on the rocks did not do justice to the true horror of this creature.

Deep-set crimson eyes, raging with the intensity of freshly lit hellfire, stared at him. The horn on the top of the creature's head was sharp, large, and stained red. Was that from the blood of all its victims? Was that his blood? The scales that covered its body were thick, like armor. They would be impenetrable to any weapon Asani could think of. The creature was broad, rivaling hippos Asani had seen in the wild. It was long as well. He guessed at least eighteen feet. Razor-sharp teeth backed up two distinctive white fangs. Even the creature's tail, which had a barb, reminding Asani of those on scorpions, had evolved with the purpose of killing.

Asani screamed, knowing it was pointless. The villagers were too far away, partying, and enjoying Mwamba's win.

Asani threw the skull he held at the Dingonek, but he didn't have the strength required, and it plopped into the river a few feet from him.

The Dingonek sprang forward and landed just before the water's edge. It swung its scorpion-like tail.

Asani couldn't dodge in time, and the blow sent him flailing through the air, where he crashed into the trunk of a tree. He heard one of his arms snap before dropping to the hard, unforgiving earth. The hurt became so unbearable, it was almost as if it couldn't be real. Sharp stabs of pain appeared randomly all over his body.

A stinging bite, from one of his feet, spiked next.

Fighting against blacking out, Asani discerned the sky above shifting. The beast dragged him somewhere. When he felt the water over his feet, he knew he was about to become sustenance for the creature of the river.

The Dingonek was real.

He had failed the ritual.

It was heartbreaking enough that he couldn't pass and that he would die, but what crushed his heart further was the fact that he would not see Fahimah again, nor have the village celebrate him.

Soon, another member of the tribe would retrieve his very skull when passing the ritual.

Asani had to accept it.

His head was now below the surface. The Dingonek was taking him deeper into the river. His lungs burned. He had to breathe. The water tasted like metal as it filled his lungs.

His view darkened.

By attempting the ritual, with or without his uncle's permission, he had already become a member of the tribe.

Not everyone could be the hero.

Some had to die for there to be skulls.

This was the way of his people.

KARMA

Doctor Michael Carrington marched into the waiting area. It wasn't often he noticed the sterilized smell or the generic seaside paintings separated by otherwise barren white walls. The hospital had become more home than home. He pulled out a chair. The *screech* caused the man seated near him to jump. Nurse Claire had told him the man's name was Bill Wheeler.

Time was scarce, and Michael chose to forgo introducing himself. "They tell me she was found on-site, covered in waste?"

Bill scratched his dark beard. The white light shining on them accentuated the wrinkles on his sunburned face. "Yes. We don't know how she got there. The place has electric fencing all around and security guards stationed at the entrance."

"Yes, but I'm not interested in that. I want to know what happened to her and what chemicals she may have been exposed to."

"I, uh."

"'Uh' can't help me. Tell me what you know, now."

"I was having lunch, and, well, I left the designated area where us guys were meant to sit and eat. That's against protocol. You won't tell, will you?"

"Just carry on."

"All right. So, I wandered around one of the older dump sites. And there she was lying on the ground, all covered in dirt, at site H. I ran to help her—and that's when I saw the green muck all over her. It hit me that she'd been exposed to the waste." Bill exhaled. "I rushed her to one of the decontamination rooms—she was so light, barely weighed anything. I—I then, brought her—"

"Bill, I'm not worried how you got her here. I want to know what harmful substances she may have encountered."

Bill's head dropped a touch, while tears swelled in his reddened eyes. "It can't be. I mean, we bury that shit so deep."

"Could she have been exposed somewhere else and stumbled to that area?"

"No. No, I didn't see any footprints on the ground. It's as if she came up through the earth, through all the waste and dirt. That or she magically appeared there."

Michael sighed. He needed to try another line of questioning.

A slender man wearing a pale-gray suit strode toward them. The man's face had a striking bronze complexion. A fake tan, no doubt, as it lacked the usual healthy glow. He had combed his chestnut-brown hair into a neat side-path.

The man paused and looked at his smartphone's screen.

He made a straight line for Bill.

"Bill Wheeler?"

Bill's eyes widened. "Yes, that's me."

"I'm Charles Penn," the man said, placing his phone into his jacket's inner pocket. "I'm here on behalf of the Rubbec Company, primarily the waste division in this area—your employers."

Bill stood, holding out his right hand.

Charles paid him no attention. His gaze had shifted to Michael. "And you are?"

"I'm Doctor Michael Carrington. I am overseeing the patient your man brought in."

"I see," Charles said, turning. "Let's go, Mister Wheeler."

"Hang on." Michael jumped to his feet. "I have questions I need answered concerning the patient."

Charles didn't stop. "I'll be around tomorrow to answer any questions. Mister Wheeler is required at the offices. Company policy. Feel free to phone and inquire, if you wish."

Bill followed the man, but turned to give Michael an awkward wave while mouthing the words, "I'm sorry."

Michael bit his tongue.

* * *

Michael entered the patient's room, taken aback by a shadowy figure slouched forward on a chair near her bedside. The person must have closed the curtains, and his eyes narrowed in the dim light of the room. He recognized her.

"Nurse Claire, is everything all right?"

No response, but Claire's left hand massaged her forehead, while in her other hand she held a clipboard on her lap.

Michael stepped forward. "Claire?"

"Ah, Doctor Carrington. Sorry, I felt a little odd."

Michael reached for the clipboard. "Let me see."

He scanned it over. "No first name? Surname? Any identification yet?"

"I don't know."

"Well, I've alerted the authorities. We'll get answers."

"Okay, Doctor."

"Nurse Claire, are you sure everything is okay?"

Claire dropped both hands into her lap and glanced at the patient in the bed, before returning her gaze to Michael. Her cheeks were void of their usual rosy color. Her mouth opened, but no words came out.

"Claire?"

"Something—something happened."

"You mean to the woman? We know that."

"No." Claire shifted in her seat. "When I came in to check on her, well, I know this sounds crazy, but there were tattoos covering her body. They were all over. I couldn't resist. I touched one on her forearm—"

"Tattoos? Of what?"

"Life," Claire said, looking at Michael. "There were animals, plants, and trees. They were magnificent."

Michael shrugged. "Claire, this woman's skin is whiter than a milk bottle and is covered in scars and blemishes. She has no tattoos."

"I know, but they were there. And when I touched one, there was a flash of light, a bright white light. The next thing I saw was a little girl in a red riding hood. We were sitting in a place I could only describe as, well, like drawings you always see of the Garden of Eden. Yes, that's what I thought when I saw the place. It was beautiful. We spoke, the little girl and I, but all I can remember was her telling me she wanted to see you. I blinked, and I was back in the room, lying on the floor. And she"—Claire looked at the patient—"she was back to normal, if you can call that normal."

Michael tapped his fingers against the clipboard. "Claire, I know this patient is unique, and I understand her appearance can be difficult to take in, but we're professionals. You should go take a break in the staff lounge. I'll be along shortly, and we can continue this talk."

"Okay, Doctor Carrington."

Claire left the room, and it seemed as if each step took a great deal of effort.

When she had closed the door behind her, Michael turned to the patient.

Once he had moved to her side, he inspected the IVs in her arms, glanced at the nasal cannula entering her nostrils, and then stared at the powder-blue blanket covering her lower half.

Finally, he looked at her.

It was hard to believe her frail appearance was due only to the waste. She looked beaten and ravaged by many hard years and various illnesses. She was bald, and her glassy eyes had no light behind them. The irises were white, as if someone had replaced her eyes with two white marbles. Her pallid skin, with its deep scars and dark blemishes all over, held the tale of much pain. Closer inspection revealed her labored breathing, reminding Michael of chain-smokers. It also revealed areas of skin stained yellow, while rashes were appearing in sensitive areas.

The scent of ammonia was apparent above the woman's face. He had to consider adding both liver and kidney failure to the list of concerns.

A cold draft drifted across the room.

Michael halted his inspection and glanced at the window—closed. He returned to the patient, noticing a dark circular mark, possibly done by a black ink pen, on her right wrist. He ran his index finger around the mark. "What is this?" he mumbled.

The patient's hand lifted. Michael froze.

Before he could rationalize what he saw, the hand closed around his right wrist.

"Hey, let go."

He looked at the woman's face, but she remained lost in her catatonic state. He tried to pry his hand free with his left hand, but it was to no avail since her grip was too tight. The mark lightened, and lime-green lines shot up her arm. Blurry pictures formed all over her limb along the lines. The lines continued to spread over her body.

Concern turned to curiosity.

He pulled her gown down with his free hand, following a few of them. The pictures formed over chest too. The lines, however, had turned to vines, darkening as the fuzzy images cleared. A plethora of colorful animals, plants, and trees became visible on the pale canvas of her upper body.

Nurse Claire's statement of seeing tattoos suddenly made sense as he struggled to take in all the beautiful, lifelike designs his eyes forced upon him. He saw an African elephant, a polar bear, and even located a giant panda. His gaze shifted, and he spotted roses and violets of the age-old poem. He glanced at a cypress tree and then an oak tree—both reminded him of his childhood neighborhood. A surge of current entered his hand from hers. Before he could summon strength for another attempt to escape, a white light exploded in the room.

His eyes fluttered.

* * *

"Doctor, are you all right?"

The sun beamed from high above in the pellucid sky and onto the lush green hills in the distance. It occurred to Michael he was lying on his back. "Where am I?"

"You're seeing one of the few remaining places on earth untouched by the hands of man."

Michael sat up. A little girl stood a few feet in front of him, her red riding hood dancing under the spell of a zephyr. "But how did I get here? I was in the hospital."

"Oh, you are a l-o-o-o-ong way from there, but we don't have a lot of time," she said. "You come across as a good man. Are you a good man, Doctor Carrington?"

"I'm a confused man is what I am." Michael rubbed his head, expecting a bump. "Did I pass out in the hospital? Am I dreaming this?"

"You ask too many unnecessary questions."

"I must've passed out. Surely, I'll awake at any moment—"

"Stop it." The little girl frowned, shaking her head. "Doctor Carrington, you must pay attention. You and your kind are hurting this world—this once-beautiful world, and along with it, me."

"Man, I must've fallen hard." Michael stared beyond the girl. A wide, deep forest spread out a few hundred yards behind her. Sounds of life emanated from the green world. What animals, and what fauna and flora, existed deeper within intrigued him. Though he could see branches swaying, guided by a breeze, the world around him had a warm atmosphere.

"You need to listen, Doctor Carrington." The girl stepped closer.

"You are the girl Nurse Claire saw."

"Nurse Claire saw me as she wanted to see me, no doubt influenced by a fairy tale of her past, it seems. You see me the same because you're influenced by her view. I look quite different, but that's of little importance."

The little girl sighed. "I am going to give you one chance to save the bad man you saw today by getting him to close the place where I was found at once, or he will be punished. Do you understand?"

"You're saying you're the woman in the bed? And the bad man is Charles Penn? Who works for the Rubbec Company?"

"Yes, yes, and yes. I'm so glad you understand."

"You must be kidding. Even if I'm not losing my mind, he'll never listen to some random doctor."

"Then he will be punished." The girl ran her hand through the empty air before her, glancing at the sun. "Things are only getting worse, I'm afraid; and if things don't become right, the only way forward will be without humans. That would be a shame."

The girl held up her hands. "Don't you see? The world around you is dying. Deforestation, the extinction of animals, the constant and many ways your kind finds to pollute the ocean and the atmosphere. Oh, how I could go on. Your kind began phasing out chlorofluorocarbons when they realized the damage being done to the ozone, but that was a drop in the ocean, as your saying goes. Why can't they see they have to act now?"

"I don't know how I could help, even if this were real. I'm just one man."

"Yes, but many 'just one man' put together could make a lot. You are not the first I've come to see. I've seen many over the years, but unfortunately, most disappoint me. And you're lucky, as many people don't even receive warnings."

Michael got to his feet. "Listen, I've had enough. I want to wake up now."

"You have twenty-four hours to convince the bad man to close the bad place, or he will experience a punishment much worse than death. He'll live the vision he brings."

Michael shook his hands. A tingling sensation had erupted around his fingers. "You're cra—"

* * *

The hospital room's white light flickered above.

Michael stood, realizing he had been lying on the floor of the patient's room. Drenched in sweat, his shirt stuck to his body. He sat on the seat that Claire had occupied, trying to find equilibrium as his mind raced for answers. He considered he'd blacked out and imagined it all, but everything had appeared so real, as if he'd truly been there. His brain demanded answers, rational answers.

He forced his eyes up, fearful of examining the patient, scared something strange might happen again. She lay as she had been when he'd first seen her. He massaged his forehead and stood, then took a few tentative steps toward her, careful not to get too close. There were no tattoos. The mark by her wrist had also vanished.

He headed to the nurses' station, anxious to see Claire, and in his mind made a list of all the further tests he wanted done on the patient. If the Rubbec Company's waste site had in any way caused the woman's current predicament, he would find out. These procedural thoughts helped contain the deeper questions concerning what had happened to him in the room.

He couldn't block out what the girl had said about Charles Penn, however, but he had no intention of mentioning anything to him. The authorities could handle him if they found any foul play or culpability due to the disposing of illegal waste. He ran his fingers around his head while he waited for one of the nurses to contact Claire and was surprised to find he had no bump after waking on the floor.

"Can't do any harm," he muttered, setting an alarm on his watch—an alarm that would go off in twenty-four hours.

* * *

The next day, Michael was stuck in meetings most of the morning. It wasn't until after lunch that he checked in on the patient who had caused him a restless night's sleep. Her condition remained unchanged. He looked over her wrist. No tattoos appeared, and no strange light exploded within the room either. He couldn't help but ponder the girl's warning, but the fear of Charles labeling him a madman extinguished any ideas of approaching him.

Claire might understand his situation.

He needed to ask her if any results had returned for the tests he'd requested. More importantly, he wanted to learn more of her dream of the girl. He had been too late searching for her yesterday, as she'd already left work.

Claire, however, proved difficult to find.

He could've asked one of the other nurses for any early results, but after their similar experiences, he only cared to see Claire. Having convinced himself their passing-out episodes were due to the trauma of seeing the woman's condition, he hoped the warning for Charles was simply his mind seeking a way to punish those he assumed were responsible. Still, the woman's state had a bigger effect on him than he first accepted. The sooner he solved what was wrong with her, the better.

After patrolling the seemingly never-ending white-walled corridors, he walked with intent to the staff lounge. He found it empty and decided he would head back to the nurses' station and get someone to call Nurse Claire.

He exited the lounge, only to feel a tug on his coat.

"Doctor Carrington."

He turned around. Nurse Claire, panting with reddened cheeks, stood before him.

"Where have you been?" he asked. "I've been looking for you. We should talk about—"

"I tried. I tried to stop him."

"Stop who?"

The beeping of his watch's alarm interrupted them. Michael switched it off. "Charles Penn," he muttered.

"Yes, how'd you know? He came here with a camera and demanded to see the patient. I was on my way to get security when I bumped into you."

Michael pushed past Claire, sprinting for the patient's room.

Claire's shoes *clack*ed behind him.

When he reached the patient's door, he signaled for Claire to stay back.

He entered, then closed the door behind him.

There was no sign of Charles. An object stuck out in his peripheral vision, however. He kneeled and picked up the camera, shaking his head. Why had Charles left it behind?

He looked at the patient. Something was off.

The patient was gone, but in her place lay Charles Penn. Michael gasped. Tendons tightened around the base of his neck.

He scanned the room. "Where is she?"

His gaze returned to Charles, and he decided to check on the man's vital signs, not trusting the machines hooked up to him. He held Charles' wrist. Before he could find a pulse, he saw the mark, in the same spot as he had seen the woman's, except this one was a deep red. Burned flesh invaded his sense of smell.

The mark shimmered as he stared at it.

Red tendrils appeared and shot up Charles' arm.

Michael tried to step away, but a blast of energy entered him as a red light erupted in the room.

The light faded to black.

* * *

"Get up, you son of a bitch."

A massive dark cloak hung across Michael's view. When he turned his neck, an active volcano rumbled in the distance. Hot lava flowed down its sides, while above, black clouds of smoke blanketed the sky. He inhaled the heavy air.

"You did this, you no-good bastard."

Michael stood, searching for the person who belonged with the voice. Ten yards from him, Charles Penn battled to free himself from an ash-colored bush, which Michael assumed was riddled by sharp thorns due to all the bleeding cuts on Charles' naked upper body.

"What's going on?" Michael asked.

Charles managed to pull himself free. "You tell me. I was taking a photo of that stupid woman, and then she grabbed me and I'm here. Did you inject me with something or knock me out?"

Michael didn't reply and stepped to Charles, who was pulling what remained of his shirt from the bush.

"Careful," Charles said. "Look down."

The ground was black, lifeless, but pockets of coals graced areas of otherwise barren earth.

"You don't have a drink, by any chance?" Charles asked.

"A what?"

"Something to drink. I've been thirsty for quite some time. I saw a pond or something a little while ago, but it was black sludge, and it smelled like shit."

"'Quite some time'? But you've been here a few minutes."

"Minutes? Sure doesn't feel that short."

Michael surveyed the lands around him. "Where are we?"

"I'd have guessed hell. But now, I'm thinking I must've passed out in the hospital room and this is all a dream. So, you're also an illusion, right?"

"I tried to convince myself I'd blacked out too."

Apart from the volcano, there was nothing but the blackened sky above and lands that seemed as if they had been on the losing end of a scorched-earth policy. His nostrils burned when he inhaled, while an acrid taste had surfaced in his mouth. Even with the lava in the distance and coals over parts of the land, the air held a frigid chill.

"I came to a place," Michael said. "When I saw her the first time, she grabbed me, but it wasn't anything like this. She said yours would be more of a vision. It might be my fault you're here."

"What are you talking about? This a trick? Did you drug me? I swear I will sue you and the piece-of-shit hospital—"

"No, it's not that. There was a little girl, and I was meant to tell you to get the company you work for to stop all the waste operations and close."

Charles spat black gunk onto the ground. He was wheezing. "Are you out of your mind? Stop a multimillion-dollar operation because of a dream?"

"It's not a dream, exactly. I'm not sure. I mean— I didn't think, couldn't think— How was I to know it was real?" A tingling sensation danced over Michael's hands. "Oh, shit, I feel it again. I'm going back. I'll try and find her."

"No, wait!" Charles screamed. "You have to wake me up. Wake me up, you son of a—"

* * *

"Doctor Carrington, are you all right?"

Michael opened his eyes. Claire stood above him.

"I'm—I'm fine," he said, getting to his feet.

"Did you see her there? The little girl."

"No, I saw him."

Claire focused on Charles. "What's wrong with him?"

"It's a coma, of sorts. No, to be honest, it's worse. I believe he's now forced to live a kind of nightmare vision as punishment. He's not here. He's somewhere else."

Claire moved toward Charles. "I knew my vision was real," she said, reaching out.

"Wait, don't touch him. It might not be safe, and we have to find the woman."

"But how on earth did she leave? She's so sick."

"Shit, Claire, I don't know, but she's the only one who can do anything for him. No medicine or procedures will do shit."

Michael left the room, heading for the nurses' station. He needed to ask the nurse on duty if she had seen a woman walk by, and he would have to alert security. Whether the company Charles worked for was damaging the environment or not, no man deserved the nightmare in which he had seen Charles.

Lost in thought, he almost crashed into a woman ahead of him, but got his arms out in front of himself in time, instinctively gripping her shoulders.

The woman didn't flinch.

"I'm so sorry." Michael inhaled an earthy fragrance with a hint of citrus.

"That's okay, Doctor," she said. "Is everything all right?"

Michael froze, captivated by the woman's beauty. Her green dress wrapped snugly around her hourglass body. She was fair skinned, and her ample breasts peered out the top of the dress' neckline, while her soft brunette hair flowed to her shoulders. Her full lips formed a smile as her emerald-green eyes softened. Whether it was instinct or not, Michael wasn't sure, but he glanced at the woman's wrist. He could have sworn he had seen the faintest remains of a tattoo.

Had the sight of Charles in the nightmare land and the other inexplicable experiences caused him to see things that weren't there? He wanted to take another look at the woman's wrist, but she had turned her arm around.

He couldn't let it go.

"I'm sorry, miss, do you mind—"

Someone tugged on his shirt.

Claire appeared alongside him. "I can't find her anywhere. Have you asked the nurse at the station?"

"One sec," Michael said, turning back to the woman.

She was gone.

A middle-aged man wearing a navy-blue shirt, with his sleeves rolled up revealing thick forearms, bustled toward them.

"Are you Doctor Carrington?" the man asked.

"Yes, that's me," Michael said. He whispered to Claire, "Keep on looking."

Claire turned and shuffled down the corridor.

"How can I help you?" Michael asked the man.

"I'm Detective Holland." The man held up his badge. "I need to see the woman you mentioned when calling in yesterday, immediately."

"We don't know where she is. Something has happened."

"You're saying she's not here?"

"She was, but she disappeared."

"Hang on." Holland took out his cell.

Michael couldn't make out the entire conversation, as Holland had walked off, but he deduced more officers were on the way. Did they already know of Charles' situation? A nurse or other staff member at the hospital may have already alerted the authorities, but he couldn't understand why the detective hadn't inquired about him. Maybe the detective had been keen to apprehend the woman first?

"Should I take you to Mister Charles Penn?" Michael asked when Holland had finished the call and returned to stand in front of him.

"Charles Penn?" Holland said, furrowing his brow.

"Aren't you here because of him?"

"No, I'm here because of Bill Wheeler. It should be all over the news by now."

"Bill Wheeler? I'm confused."

"He brought in the woman yesterday?"

"Yeah."

"Well, during the lunch break at the Rubbec Company's waste site today, he managed to blow over half the place to shit. Luckily no serious injuries. Most of the employees were in the few areas he didn't target. He gave himself up, and he's since been mumbling about the woman he brought here yesterday."

Holland leaned in closer. His voice dropped in volume. "Apparently, she visited him during the night and told him the place had to be destroyed. He did an excellent job too, seeing as the company will surely close up for good in this area. They've had a lot of trouble come their way the last while."

Michael rubbed his forehead. "That's—that's crazy."

"You're telling me. I thought you informed the officers yesterday that she was in a coma or something?"

"Yeah, she was."

Holland frowned. "That's odd. Well, we've put out her description. I can't imagine she'll get too far looking the way she does, but we need to search around here, and then we can finish this discussion."

"I have to show you Charles first. He was the Rubbec Company's lawyer."

"What's wrong with him?"

"Let me show you."

"Lead the way."

Michael's mind spun as if thrown in a blender, and he had to piece together shredded thoughts. The woman must have given Bill an ultimatum, similar to the one she had given him. Except Bill had followed through, and he hadn't. Bill would get off after a few years, as there were no injured, and everyone in town hated the place anyway. To many, Bill would even be a hero. They would petition for an early release, and the community would care for him. As for himself, Michael would have to endure knowing it was his inaction that had seen Charles punished. He would have to live with that forever. He doubted anyone could help Charles.

In twenty-four hours, his world had flipped upside down. How would he explain it all to the detective? It was best to leave out the strange vision he'd had and the trip to Charles' hell. He would speak to Claire before she spoke to the police, to convince her to do the same.

As for the woman, he doubted they would ever find her. There was something different about her, something *not* human. What he knew for sure, however, was this woman with the love for all things nature, its guardian, grew ever more restless.

He pitied whoever ran into her next.

SHAPES IN THE WATER

Sirens whined. Dexter Ford knew well-trained special ops forces aided by night-vision goggles were on their trail. These forces had permission to kill if left with no other recourse. Teams would have deployed to defend the target while other units hunted them.

He knew this because moments ago, he had still been one of them.

His brother Michael, who had discharged himself from the same force, crashed into him, sending him to the ground.

"Shit, Dex. I told you to stay low."

Beams from the base's towering searchlights missed them as they followed an almost nonexistent path toward the edge of the cliff. Around them various knee-high bushes made movement slow, while farther away, tall trees stood guard. This had been the only way, even if it was the most treacherous, to reach their goal.

Dexter pushed up onto his knees.

"We've got to be careful. Otherwise it's special court-martialing for nothing," Michael said. "And you know what would happen to us—we'd be locked away forever. Everyone in this force knows the risks."

"Sorry," Dexter said.

Michael checked the time on his wristwatch. "We gotta get a move on, and keep as low as possible."

Dexter looked at the starry sky, which was excellent for navigation but bad for stealth operations. He'd wanted to pack bags with sufficient supplies, but time had been against them. All they managed to take was what they could carry. This boiled down to their weapons, flashlights, a first-aid pack, some snacks, their knives, and two canteens of water. They headed into the unknown unprepared.

Michael asked, "What's our primary goal?"

"Find cover, assess the situation, find Travis, and get the fuck out."

"That's right."

"Michael, are we sure there is a way out?"

"Yeah... We'll find it." Michael pointed ahead. "The cliff's edge is right there. I don't think they know we've come this way yet. It's a bit daring."

Dexter clenched his gun; he didn't want to have to use it against people he had known for so long.

Michael crept forward, motioning with his hand for Dexter to follow. Dexter obeyed. The movements were sluggish at first, but he soon found a workable rhythm while one eye continued to scan for any men coming out of the line of trees in the distance.

At the cliff's edge, they resorted to crawling like snakes.

Dexter peered over, cautious of the troops below, who had set up on the riverbanks. The troops were all on red alert. So much as a glimpse of him and his brother, and the firing of weapons would commence. His vision blurred. It all seemed surreal, as if he had shifted into a parallel reality. He thought of his brother Travis. There could be no going back.

"It's really high," Dexter said.

"It's the only way," Michael said, glancing below. "See how they've already secured the entire area down there? Soon they'll have men here as well." Michael paused, his breathing audible. "Now, see the river below us?"

"Yeah. Oh shit, is that it?"

"Yes."

Below them, a dark circle appeared to hover on the surface of the river. It was a strange mixture of purple-and-black streaks. It shimmered every few moments.

"The wormhole," Dexter muttered. "It's a big jump. You sure we won't be injured?"

"Dex, it's hard to explain, but from what I heard during the briefing, you won't be hitting the water at all. When you hit that thing, you end up somewhere else."

Dexter's world had taken a strange turn when Michael had come to fetch him. The story his brother told him had caused his brain to shudder; such was the massive amount of bizarre information he needed to process. Their force had rushed out here due to another of those things appearing, this time over an unnamed river in California. Their brother Travis and two soldiers had entered one more than a year ago, and the wormhole disappeared before they could return. Any intel from that operation or the current one was on a need-to-know basis, and the consequences were severe for those who even dared to whisper a word. Michael had shattered protocol when he told Dexter all he'd heard during the emergency briefing.

Travis had been the only scientist in the three-man expedition force sent into the wormhole, which mysteriously opened above Lake Champlain back then. It had been a traversable wormhole, allowing the team to transmit information back. They described the world painted in pastels of purple and pink. No flora or fauna were apparent, but water was abundant. One of the men had started shouting, and then the wormhole closed, severing any connection to the team.

Michael was desperate to search for their brother. The commanders denied such an expedition, saying the men were probably dead, and that they couldn't guarantee this wormhole would take them wherever the three men had gone. They didn't even know if the current wormhole was traversable.

Michael had begged for reconsideration.

That had been his first warning of a court-martialing. He faked calmness and eventually returned to the barracks. There he found Dexter...

Dexter cleared his mind. There was no use worrying over what had happened already. He took another glance at the river below. "We don't even know what we're up against. How will only the two of us be able to find Travis?"

"We have no other choice. He'd have done the same for us," Michael said, looking at Dexter. "Trust me."

Dexter nodded.

"Remember, we find cover and weigh up what we're dealing with."

Dexter nodded again, this time with more force.

"You go first," Michael said.

Dexter crawled back and stood. The target was sizeable, and it wasn't the stress of missing it that concerned him, but what would happen if it simply vanished. Michael had tried to make him understand how serious things would be on the other side, yet the other world still seemed too unreal to awaken much fear in him.

"Go," Michael said.

Dexter ran for the edge and jumped.

The wormhole appeared beneath his feet. He had successfully aimed right for its center and braced himself for impact, still unsure what was to come. He heard voices, loud, and the cacophony of gunfire, and hoped Michael would get through unscathed.

He hit the wormhole.

No hard impact came, nor was there a splash.

* * *

The initial blackness gave way to rushing lights. Explosions of color followed. Intricate patterns formed, dancing all around him. An image before him cleared. Dexter found himself hurtling across what seemed to be a type of marshland terrain. The ground was soft, springy, and wet.

When he came to a stop, he rolled over, got onto his haunches. His gun was ready to fire, and he ignored that he was near soaked. He would have been ill from the nausea that came from the traveling and from fear for Michael's chances to make it through safely, but the world around him commanded all his attention.

There were rivers and streams everywhere, not relegated to the magenta-colored ground. A few seemed to travel midair, running vertically from the ground or interconnected and stretching horizontally. Their depths and widths varied, as if they were future-age highways and roads built in the sky. Was the water, which ranged from clear to murky, contained in a type of see-through tubing? He immediately doubted this, even if logic said otherwise. Some of these strange currents of water were closed loops flowing back into large rivers or streams across the landscape. He stood, looking around, and some didn't even appear to have contact with the ground, but he figured that may have been due to his limitations in sight. He studied a few of the smaller dark streams above him. They didn't seem to have a basic structure or design as the larger rivers did. Instead, they appeared to move and develop wherever they wanted.

"What the fuck?" Dexter said, trying to understand how water obeyed different laws here.

If it is water.

He inhaled a pungent burned-rubber smell that caused him to wiggle his nose. He stepped forward, noticing his body felt lighter. The gravity was weaker than on Earth.

Where am I? Where is this place?

A *thud* came from a few feet behind him, and he turned around.

Michael was staring back at him.

Dexter said, "You got through. Were you hit?"

Michael checked over his body. "All good." He readied his weapon and returned his gaze to Dexter. "It was close though," he said, surveying the area around them. "Well, this looks like the right place. Crazy shit, huh?"

"Yeah. You didn't mention Travis or the others reporting any damn highways and byways of water overhead."

Michael looked up. "It was darker when they were here." He turned around and shrugged. "Well, even if it was a traversable wormhole, doubt we'd get up there."

Dexter tracked Michael's gaze. The wormhole was hovering twenty-five feet in the air, alongside another banner-like river of clear water that reached into the sky. Dexter looked up, following the river. It took a moment to register, but when he finally comprehended what he was seeing above, a coldness invaded his body.

"Wait. Where is the sky?" he asked.

Michael observed the heavens.

Far above them, there seemed to be a vast ocean of water instead of a sky.

"Is it a trick reflection or something?" Dexter asked.

"Nah, I don't think so. Maybe there are levels."

"Levels of water?"

"Yeah. Maybe we'd have to be above that body of water to see the sky."

"How is there light here then?"

"I don't know, Dex."

Dexter lowered his gaze and scanned the landscape. "So there's air between the layers? We're breathing it, and nothing will happen to us?"

"Yeah. Travis and his team were able to take off their masks after checking the atmosphere's composition. It was one of their last reports. It's breathable. I'd have told you if we needed oxygen, dummy."

Michael hadn't mentioned whether Travis or any of the team had reported back on this place's atmosphere. Was there anything else he should know? Dexter tensed when he recalled Michael's insistence on having weapons.

"Come on," Michael said. "Let's see if we can get a better lay of the land. If you see any shelter or something we can use as cover, let me know."

"Where? All I see is this purple...whatever this shit is and the damn water everywhere. And way over there at three o'clock, it looks like a damn ocean. We could never cross that. How deep is it?"

"The land is kind of a sponge." Michael tapped the ground with his boot. "And...if there's no cover, it's even more imperative we get in and get out, especially while we have this light. We don't know how long it will last, and journeying through this place in the dark won't be fun."

An itch broke out at the base of Dexter's neck. "Fuck, Michael. You're avoiding my questions, keeping info from me. Can you at least tell me how we're getting out?"

"No idea." Michael walked away with his gun ready for action. "I'm hoping Travis will know something."

More questions circled in Dexter's head. If Travis knew a way out, why hadn't they seen him since the day he entered this world? He bit his tongue and focused on the landscape instead.

Dexter could see far into the distance when the water did not obstruct his view, and there was nothing but the strange ground and water in any direction he looked. The ground didn't worry him too much, as his boots gripped it reasonably well. If danger of any type approached, he would see it coming in time. The clear water he also didn't mind. The darkened water, however, did cause him some unease. It had a rotting-fish stench that unnerved him even more whenever he got near it.

He saw more arms of dark water returning to narrow streams on the land.

Purple sponge and black water. How weird.

"Could any animals live in the oceans or rivers here, or hell, even the streams?" Dexter asked.

Michael glanced back. "I don't know, but let's try to keep away from any water, especially the murky stuff."

Dexter couldn't agree more.

* * *

They walked for a good twenty minutes, ever vigilant. The streams of water increased and grew more complex. Ahead, Dexter saw their first true obstacle.

Reaching all the way to the ocean in the sky was what looked like a crisscrossed fence of pitch-black water. The gaps between the water were no bigger than a human head.

"Well, we're unfortunately going to get wet," Michael said. He paused fifteen feet from the fence of water.

"We're going through?"

"Yes."

Dexter stepped closer. He tried calming himself to lower his heart rate before his adrenal gland produced too much adrenaline. He peered through one of the gaps. The fence was thin—one step and they would be through—but farther ahead, roughly a hundred and fifty yards, a massive curtain of clear water rose up.

He pulled his head back, frowning. "There's even more damn water ahead."

"Relax. We'll check it out when we get there." Michael stepped through the fence of water without warning.

On the other side, he cursed in pain.

Dexter could barely see his brother through the water, but it appeared he was leaning over. Dexter clutched his gun tight and jumped through.

"What's wrong?" Dexter asked on the other side.

"You get through okay?"

"Yes, I'm fine. You're the one going on in pain."

Michael showed Dexter his bloodied forearm. "Just a nick."

"How the hell did that happen?"

Michael didn't reply, and Dexter knelt next to his brother, opening the first-aid bag.

Cleaning the area, he assessed the damage. It was one long scratch, from below the wrist to the elbow. His brother had been fortunate; deeper and they would have serious problems.

Dexter disinfected and bandaged the wound. "What did this?"

Michael stood. "Well, there are," he said as he turned around to face Dexter, "some things…"

"Michael?" Dexter asked. His brother had frozen in place.

Michael became reanimated and pushed him back.

Dexter didn't have time to react and fell onto the ground.

"Stay down!" Michael said, diving alongside him.

Dexter looked at where he had been standing. A stream of dark water had smashed through the fence of water they'd negotiated and now ran across the space. He looked back to see where it may have come from. His assumption was correct: it emanated from a darkening spot in the massive wall of clear water he had seen.

Michael rolled underneath the stream. "Come on," he said. "Try not to touch the water."

Dexter followed, crawling beneath the stream; Michael, impatient, clutched his arms and pulled him out. On his feet, Dexter felt a tug on his shoulder. Was it his brother? Turning around, he glimpsed smooth black tentacles retreating into the stream.

"What the fuck was that?" Dexter asked.

"No time for questions. We gotta run."

"What? Why?"

Michael turned Dexter's head to the wall of water. It was moving toward them. Tendril-like streams shot out in all directions, and Dexter could see black shapes riding along.

He followed Michael, sprinting as fast as possible while maintaining balance on the terrain. Two streams boxed them in and were closing on them. Michael opened fire, and Dexter followed suit. The things in the water screamed, sounding similar to bats, as bullets greeted them. The blurry shapes cleared. They were strange black squid-like creatures, and they came in all sizes. Some would even be able to travel in a beam of water no thicker than his arm.

Michael opened fire on the stream directly in front of him. Two black shapes fell out, but there was no time for closer inspection. He jumped through the stream, which had grown since it first appeared, and Dexter followed.

Both came through safely.

Michael dropped his gun, presumably empty, and kept running. "Keep up, Dex!"

Dexter ran. He didn't want to drop his gun, but he decided to do as his brother had, needing to be able to move as fast as possible. The weapon would be useless anyway once the wall of water hit them, and it was near, less than fifty yards. He didn't see any escape. They were going to die on this planet, torn to shreds by these abominations.

Michael vanished from his view.

Dexter sprinted to the spot where he had last seen his brother.

There was a pool of clear water, less than four feet in diameter. Michael must have fallen in. He turned to look at the wall of water, and his eyes widened.

He could see the shapes of giant, dinosaur-like creatures in areas of clear water. They were under attack from thousands of the squid creatures, shrouded in clouds of darker water. The sight rivaled epic space-opera battles, and he had a massive screen on which to view it. He needed to move, but his body remained stiff as if paralysis had gripped it.

Only when the wall reached him did he budge.

He jumped into the pool of water.

* * *

The pool of water had been as thin as a sheet of paper. Dexter remained falling.

Fortunately, more of the spongy ground cushioned his landing.

"'Bout time," Michael said.

The beam of Michael's flashlight found Dexter's face.

Dexter searched for his flashlight, but it was gone, and so was the first-aid bag. He clenched his teeth, preventing himself from swearing out loud. "Where are we?"

"A kind of tunnel."

"Did you see those things?"

"The plesiosaur-looking things?"

"Yeah, I guess—they kinda look like dinosaurs."

"That's them." Michael's voice softened. "Listen, Dex. I have bad news." He shone the flashlight on his hand.

Dexter saw a dog tag. "Travis?"

"Yeah. I found what's left of him over there." Michael directed his flashlight beam deeper into the tunnel, but all Dexter saw was more darkness. "He had the other guys' tags with him. He must have been the last to go," Michael said, bringing the flashlight to a notebook he held. Dexter glimpsed his brother's face, the pain evident.

"Catch." Michael tossed the notebook. "Have a look through it, and see if there's anything on how to get home."

Dexter tried to keep his composure like Michael. Trained to be a hardened man, he fought his aching heart, which felt as if pulled by an anchor into a bottomless sea. His brother was gone.

He shone the flashlight on the notebook, and with hands shaking, he opened the waterproof bag protecting it.

He took out the notebook.

"You can read it while we walk," Michael said. "We gotta find an exit back to the level above us."

Dexter didn't move.

"Now, Dex," Michael said, raising his voice. "Our mission is complete. We know what happened to Travis. It's time to get the fuck home."

Dexter fell in behind Michael. They headed the opposite direction, away from where Michael had seen Travis' remains. Gradually it appeared as though they were moving upward.

The notebook had a few pages of scribbled notes, and Dexter couldn't believe what he read. Travis first stated he believed the planet was actually an organism capable of opening wormholes throughout the universe and that the plesiosaurs lived in symbiosis with it. They would travel through the wormholes, visiting worlds that had water, and when they returned, the organism would read their minds and extract the data they brought back. Images for inspection, smells for study—to work out the composition of atmospheres?—and sounds to playback.

But to what end? And how many times have they visited Earth?

He remembered the tales of Champ, the monster that apparently lived in Lake Champlain, the same lake where the first wormhole—that he knew of—had appeared. And what of Nahuelito, the plesiosaur-like animal that legend said lived in Nahuel Huapi Lake, Patagonia, Argentina?

Travis also said the plesiosaurs ate the squid creatures for sustenance, which helped the organism, as the squids were harmful to it if left uncontrolled.

On this planet—or organism—the battle appeared lost. The squid creatures were taking over and had turned the tide against the plesiosaurs. The organism was dying, slowly, as if the squid creatures had become its own form of cancer.

Travis' main fear was that these creatures would soon discover the wormholes opening to other worlds, if they hadn't already. He also warned the wormholes would be open for less and less time as the organism grew more ill. The final sentence mentioned he and the two soldiers had been searching for one. Dexter's core twisted, as he knew they had never found a way out.

Dexter bumped into an obstacle. He lifted his flashlight, ready to strike.

"Watch it," Michael said.

He relaxed, realizing it was his brother.

"We're here." Michael pointed up.

Another circular pool of water was situated above them. It was close enough that one brother could lift the other, then have the other pull him up.

Dexter hoped nothing awaited them.

* * *

After Michael peered out and confirmed there was no present danger, they left the safety of the tunnel. Fortune smiled upon them—less than a hundred yards away, a sphere with shades of blue and white hovered above a clear stream of water that ran on the surface. The major concern was to where it led.

Was the organism trying to help?

Surely that's madness.

Travis' notes had caused a tilt in the way Dexter viewed things, but he couldn't be sure of his brother's mental state when he had written them.

His chest felt heavy.

Another problem presented itself. Two walls of water towered on either side of them, and ominous black shapes lurked behind murky clouds.

Michael pulled out his knife. "Hand me yours."

Dexter, unsure why he would want two knives, complied nevertheless.

"Take the dog tags out of my pocket. Keep them and the notebook safe."

Dexter did as instructed, ignoring the knots in his stomach.

"Right. Now, I want you to run along the stream and dive for that wormhole. No matter what happens, you don't stop. Do you understand?"

"Does it take us home?"

"Let's hope, but any place is better than this shit hole."

"And you?"

"I'll be behind you." Michael stood, a knife in each hand. "Now go," he shouted.

Dexter ran.

The walls closed in.

He got the sense the organism could no longer control the water; he figured one day the entire place would drown, and the squid creatures would reign until they had devoured all they could. He heard Michael running behind him, which helped fuel him to go faster.

We can do this. We can make it.

When Dexter had less than fifty feet to go, a black tentacle burst out of the wall to his left, but before it could latch onto him, something stopped it. He glanced to his side and caught a glimpse of the head of one of the plesiosaurs sticking out of the wall of water. The plesiosaur had one of the squids in its mouth. He glanced to his other side, and another plesiosaur shape flanked him. The organism must be trying to help.

All thoughts ceased.

Dexter jumped into the wormhole.

* * *

This time Dexter did hit water—a lot of water. He made for the surface, turned onto his back in an attempt to float, and hoped the notebook in its bag against his chest wouldn't suffer any damage. Above him, a pale-blue sky stretched across his view, and even though the sun hid behind gray clouds, he knew the heavens well.

He was home.

He eased his neck up, careful so as not to lose his balance on the water's surface, and looked toward the wormhole. He hoped to see his brother come through.

Michael didn't join him.

The wormhole flickered, fading with each passing second. Finally, it collapsed within itself and vanished. Dexter wanted to surrender to the large body of water, which must be a type of lake.

The initial chill in its currents had passed as his body numbed.

He fought back tears, hoping and praying Michael would find another way out. The idea of losing two brothers to that place hurt like a thousand needles to the heart. The only warmth that swept through his body came from the realization that if the other planet was dying, so too would those black abominations.

Earth will be safe. Or will it?

He considered the idea some of them may have already come through. Or had the plesiosaurs been gatekeepers as well as explorers? His mind hurt as he ran through the possibilities. One thought stuck: His brothers wouldn't die in vain. He would get the notebook to the right people. Even if no wormhole opened again, the right authorities would at least have a theory regarding any that had.

The world would know of his brothers and their sacrifices.

* * *

Unsure as to how long he had been floating, Dexter decided to find shore, bracing through another wave of concern for Michael. He looked to his sides, trying to spot the nearest land. A peculiar accent broke the silence.

"Well, I'll be. Two in one day. I'm sure as hell going to be the talk of the town tonight."

Dexter looked back, to his left. An old man with a large gray beard, wearing a blue hat, was approaching in his rowboat. Dexter couldn't place the accent, but it was not American. He tried to reply, but the words didn't come.

The man helped him onto the boat, where Dexter collapsed.

The man stood, towering above him. "Lad, are you okay? The other one was as beat up as you. Well, maybe a tad more beat up, but I got him to shore, only for him to come 'round and refuse treatment. Gone straight back out with Fred in the motorboat to look for a fellow. I said I'd help, came this way. Guess you're the fellow, unless there are more of you floating around?"

"Michael? My brother, you found him?"

"Sure did, a little while ago. He'll be fine."

Dexter sat up. New energy pumped through his body.

Michael was safe.

"Where the hell am I?" Dexter muttered.

"You're in Loch Ness."

"Loch Ness, California? I've never heard of it."

"You're in Scotland. The country, lad." The old man spread his arms. "The home of Nessie."

THE THRONE OF SPACE AND TIME

Assistant's Note: The letter you are about to read was handed to me by my former employee, Phillip Murdoch, the esteemed historian. It was the first and last time I visited him at the institution. Out of respect to him, I've decided to follow his wish and send each of you a copy of the letter. His words are unaltered, and I hope you forgive and understand my notes.

* * *

Dear Friends,

If you are reading this, my no-good assistant has done something right for once. He promised to visit and sneak this letter out. He will then make a copy for each one of the four of you. You see, I require aid from one of you, as I currently find myself locked away in an institution. I believe one of you may have had a suspicion of my confinement already. I've no doubt, however, that soon I shall be cleared as mentally competent, that my freedom will be restored, and that I'll be allowed to continue my destiny. With your help, you noble and respected men of science, everything can be expedited.

Many leading physicists doubt whether going back in time is possible. Travelling forward in time seems achievable, theoretically at least. I confess that I, a simple historian, will not be telling you I've physically adventured into the past. Seeing the past, on the other hand, is a different matter. I don't know if my earlier calls to you were comprehensible, so this is my attempt to explain it all clearly and honestly.

My father always told me that every object had its own story to tell. I never truly knew what he meant until late one night when I decided to donate some of his old belongings to charity. I'd contacted my assistant and told him to be at my place early the next morning. I'd then made my way down into the stale, cold basement, where I kept most of my father's possessions since his passing.

After I piled various items to give away, a large black box hidden away in the far corner caught my eye. That's where I also found a body-length mirror beneath a tattered powder blue blanket. Behind the mirror was a strange cylindrical device, but my mind was zoned in on the box. With great effort, I managed to pull and slide it across the floor, until it rested under the basement's light. The word *veritas*, which you know is Latin for 'truth,' was written on its top in permanent marker.

The box's interior was a mess, with all sorts of lights, magnets, batteries, wires, cables, and other jumbled up contraptions. Scraps of paper littered the box as well. My father had clearly been in a rush when he'd packed this, and it was unlike his usual meticulousness. He'd never been completely fulfilled as a science teacher and had often played around with his experiments, much to my mother's annoyance. The thing that I found most odd was that my father had never shown me this odd contraption or what it did. He'd shown me everything else, always beaming with pride, even for the projects that failed.

I was bitten by intrigue, and it didn't take me long to find schematics scrawled on dusty, faded pages. As I found later, the mirror was to play a crucial role. I pulled it, along with the cylindrical device attached to its back, until it stood in the middle of the room. I then pushed everything, except the mirror with its device and the box, back into the shadows of the basement.

Donating to charity had been relegated to the back of my mind.

* * *

As I found more papers at the bottom of the box, I realised these components were meant to go all around the mirror. The process was long and laborious, especially for a man in his seventies, but I persevered, finishing at just after four in the morning.

As I adjusted my glasses, I studied the page in my hand. I then looked to the mirror. It now had all sorts of lights, lasers, magnets, batteries, and other peculiar devices around it. They were all connected by a plethora of different coloured wires, cables, and some other unique connections. Everything seemed to match up to the pages I held.

At the back of the mirror, I had to connect all the wires and cables to the cylindrical device. It was not until about five in the morning that I had done everything I could. After I checked the pages, I discovered I needed to place an object on the floor, so I grabbed one of my father's old shoes and placed it the correct length as shown in the diagram. Then, I flicked the switch on the back of the mirror as indicated, and slowly the cylindrical device started to hum and move up and down. A section of it began to spin. It spun ever faster then points of lights from the front of the mirror lit up the entire floor.

Realising my work wasn't done, I aligned all the lasers and lights towards the shoe. I did so, and then moved back, tapping my foot as I waited to see exactly what this strange experiment would achieve.

It took nearly ten minutes, but finally a faint glow seemed to hover around the shoe. As it grew brighter, a strange cloud, almost like dust, drifted off the shoe and headed towards the mirror. The particles in the dust cloud shimmered, and different shades of colours swirled. I wanted to laugh at this silly contraption, for I could detect no purpose. I also felt an undercurrent of sadness as I wondered how long my father had spent on this failed experiment.

"What does it do?" I asked the empty basement.

That's when I noticed the mirror begin to flicker. I took a step closer. The dust that had risen from the shoe had thinned. The mirror, however, did not display my reflection, but rather showed a massive cloud or thick fog.

An image began to form, a dark shape behind the fog. I removed my glasses and cleaned them with the cuff of my shirt, a usual habit of mine when I was puzzled. When I put them back on, the shape was still there, but it was moving. The device's humming got louder. The fog cleared. An image was now visible. It appeared no better than an old television screen, the colours terribly faded and grainy, but the mirror showed me a young man putting on a shoe.

He stood up. A cold shiver crept down my spine like a snake.

It was my father in his early thirties.

* * *

I don't know how long I stood, motionless, transfixed, but when the image flickered and darkened, I reached out with my hand.

"No," I said, but it was gone. The dark fog had replaced it.

I didn't stand desolate for long, for the fog cleared again. This time, an old man with a grey moustache appeared to be working on something. As the old man moved aside, I realised he was busy making the very shoe my father had purchased and had worn for so many years.

I couldn't believe it. My father had built a machine capable of looking back in time, at least through the objects the machine focused on. A knock on the basement door caused me to jump. I hustled for the machine's switch and flicked it off, which made it come to an immediate stop. I looked at the mirror to be sure and saw an old man with ruffled grey. His wide eyes stared back at me.

It was my reflection.

I turned to the basement door. "Who is calling so early?"

I already knew it could be only one of two people that had entry to my home but was annoyed at being disturbed and wished for them to know it.

"It's me. You said to come at six. Trust me, I wish I was still asleep," my assistant said.

I checked my wristwatch and frowned. The night had gone by so fast. At least for once my assistant had decided to show up on time. I realised why I'd asked him here today.

The donations.

I had to usher him out as fast as I could, for I didn't want him to become interested in the machine. I wasn't sure how I felt about its capabilities yet and wanted to run more experiments to be sure. I grabbed any old clothes, adding them to what I had already set aside, then gave everything to my assistant and told him to leave.

When he'd gone, it occurred to me I hadn't slept. I made my way upstairs and poured myself a stiff drink; there was no way I could sleep otherwise. I was too wired. After another drink, my mind exploded with ideas.

By the time I finished nearly half the bottle of whiskey, I was stumbling around the living area, laughing hysterically. I believed in the machine's capabilities, and it seemed I'd found my very own *eureka* moment. What I could accomplish with the machine had dawned upon me, nearly ripping my tether from the world. For so long I'd been some dusty old historian left behind by the new world of science and discovery.

"I will have the last laugh," I said aloud, toasting another drink to myself.

I had a plan, a plan that would turn me into the greatest man in all of history. Governments, famous families, celebrities, anyone and everyone would come to respect me. I could find out all the deepest secrets of human civilisation. Nothing need go unanswered, and all I would require was the object to show me the way.

Veritas, yes, truth would be mine.

I then cursed as I entertained another lane of thought. Getting some of these objects would not be easy. Imagine if one could procure a royal crown. Oh, the secrets it would tell. Or a weapon, what murders and scandals it would hide. I had to get started, but I needed to start small. I could hook smaller fish then work my way up to the big hungry sharks of our world.

Back came the joy, I danced on the spot, and spilled most of my drink. I was about to bring the world to its knees. For more than seventy years of my life I'd been a slave to the system, just another cog in the machine—

but now, now I would become its master. I would become a legend.

I sat down on my tattered brown chair, having decided to take a nap. When I awoke, I would begin to set my plan in motion.

* * *

When I opened my eyes, my assistant stood before me. I then looked down at the empty glass in my lap.

"You can snore," my assistant said. "I thought the devil had possessed you there for a moment."

"Do not make jokes of things you don't understand," I said. "What are you doing here anyway?"

"I usually come on a Sunday afternoon to help you with your research."

"Research?"

"For the historical books or series, on Rome, that you're writing. Thought you were already behind on your deadline?"

"Forget that nonsense," I said, looking at the bottle of whiskey, eager to pour a drink. I decided against it. I needed a clear head. "Let me pose a hypothetical question to you."

"I'm listening."

I studied my assistant, doubting his statement, but decided to proceed. "Say you had a machine that could look back to the history of any object. What would you want to see? Tell me something impressive and an object that you could easily lay your hands on."

"Well, no such machine could ever—"

"Use your imagination, man."

"Um, okay," my assistant said. "What about that piece of stone or whatever you have. You said that it came from one of the pyramids from Egypt. You could answer the question as to who really built the pyramids."

I shot straight up from the chair. "Brilliant. Now get out."

"What?"

"I'm not doing any research today. I'm tired. Now go," I said, ushering my assistant out of my home.

* * *

I threw myself up the stairs for the piece of limestone I'd managed to buy from an old friend, an archaeologist, who'd spent many years studying the pyramids. Once I had the little piece, I made my way down to the basement and set up the machine. My heart was beating so hard, I feared it may give in due to all the excitement.

I placed the piece of limestone on the floor, set up everything as I had before, and switched on the machine. The limestone started to glow a dim white. My hands formed tight-balled fists as I waited in anticipation.

I kept reminding myself to breathe.

The colourful dust cloud appeared.

The dark fog filled the mirror, and then it cleared. Slowly, the image showed itself. A topless, broad-shouldered and dark-skinned man with long black hair and a wild beard stood looking at a large block of limestone. He was using a handheld tool to try and level its surface. I figured that this must be the original block from which my piece had broken.

Sadness took hold, as it seemed that the boring and most realistic theory of man having built the pyramids was true. The image blurred into a haze, and when it dissipated, the limestone block had been placed upon another, which had been placed on another, this upon another. My view was limited, and I guessed this was the actual building of a pyramid. It was incredible to see, and I pushed away all negative thoughts. This was an amazing moment in history. Two men, similar to the one I'd seen levelling the limestone, got to their knees and bowed. I couldn't see who approached off screen. The energy reawakened within me. I hoped the man they revered would appear.

He did. Slowly, like an animal stalking its prey, he stood before the two men. He was tall, muscular, dark—so dark he rivalled a starless space in the night sky. He wore a strange, jackal-like mask and glanced at the two men kneeling before him. He waved his arm at them as if he were shooing away flies. They jumped up and went back to work.

"Unbelievable," I said. "This is incredible."

The tall being turned with incredible speed, and before I could blink, he was staring right at me. He wore no mask. The jackal-looking head was truly his face. His deep-set yellow eyes glared at me.

My world shuddered.

He pointed at me. I couldn't understand how he saw me. It was impossible. I tried to move, but my body locked in paralysis. The being started taking long strides towards the mirror. I needed to act, and I forced movement upon myself.

The being saw me flinch and opened his hand. A yellow orb of energy, like controlled lightning, danced in his palm. He lifted his hand, his palm facing me, and a bolt of energy shot from the orb.

It came through the mirror.

It hit me.

A tingling sensation erupted over my skin, and a strange current ran all along my veins. I cried out and ran for the piece of limestone. The being came ever closer. I feared he would come through, how, I didn't know, but after the bolt I wouldn't take the chance. I dove for the piece of limestone and knocked it away, praying the machine would close in time. As I pushed up with my arms, an ominous feeling tugged within.

I turned my head to look at the image on the mirror. It was fading, but the being had his arms outstretched and was managing to slow its closing. He spoke in a deep, booming voice. The words bounced within me, and my insides threatened to explode.

"Yes, Master, soon," I said.

The image disappeared. The mirror had gone back to reflecting this world. I was confused as to why I had spoken to him, and even more perplexed by what I'd said. I got to my feet, switched off the machine, and picked up the limestone.

I needed to keep it safe.

* * *

I won't lie. This encounter did leave me in a strange state for the rest of the day and most of the next. I came out of my daze the next evening to find I'd written the same words over and over on pieces of paper.

Anubis, true ruler of the dead.
Shall claim the throne of space and time.

The pieces of paper lay all over my living room floor. The words made no sense to me, and I dismissed them.

After a few heavy-handed drinks, I'd recovered somewhat from the harrowing experience. It's here when I contacted you four, my friends, in somewhat of a rambling state. I wish I'd been clearer in my delivery. Three of you hadn't believed me. One of you had alerted the authorities I wasn't well.

Anubis, true ruler of the dead.
Shall claim the throne of space and time.

The authorities did come, but not before I realised I needed to hide the machine, which I did. I tried to remain calm when they asked their questions, but I failed their simple tests, and the frustration at being delayed in my work caused me to act out. They grabbed me against my will and injected me with a drug. When I awoke again, I was here in this institution and now must face their pointless daily questions.

Anubis, true ruler of the dead.
Shall claim the throne of space and time.

But as you can all see, I'm well, and have even recovered from the episode. All I need is one of you to believe me, even the one who contacted the authorities. All is forgiven. Join me and together with the weapon of truth, the *veritas*, we shall become legends. Trust me, only good shall come of it.

Anubis, true ruler of the dead.
Shall claim the throne of space and time.
Please, my friends. I only need one of you to believe me.

Anubis, true ruler of the dead.
Shall claim the throne of space and time.
Together, we will be great.
Anubis, true ruler of the dead.
Shall claim the throne of space and time.
I am well.
Your friend and colleague,
Phillip Murdoch

* * *

Assistant's Note: After reading the letter during the copying process, I returned to Mister Murdoch's residence. I didn't find the machine that he spoke of. I didn't find the piece of limestone he referred to, and I deny ever having a conversation with him concerning it or a machine that could see back into the past. My search was thorough, as I know of every possible place he may have intended to hide anything. It is of my opinion that no machine ever existed.

As you can see, Mister Murdoch is very ill. He suffered a serious nervous breakdown during his research for works he intended to publish on ancient Rome. I think it is best he is left alone, as to play into his delusions will only hinder his recovery. I will play no part further in it.

HER HEART BEATS FOR ANCIENT BEASTS

Anubis, the true ruler of the dead.
Shall claim the throne of space and time.
I consider this matter closed.

FORBIDDEN FRUIT

Billions of lightbulbs, plugged into the nighttime sky, illuminated the land.

Todd Watson awoke from a power nap and wiped dots of sweat off his forehead. Summer nights in the veld offered no respite from the heat of the day. At least he had shaved his head before the trip, already aware of the humidity and warmth he would have to endure. He sat up, looked at the bottoms of his boots, and pulled out the ash-white thorns that had found home in his soles. Mouthing choice curse words at the sweat covering his body, he looked at his friend Dan Matthews. He had scolded Dan less than an hour ago for wanting to start a small fire. The agitation he'd felt at Dan's rookie stupidity dissipated as he watched his friend eating cold sausages from a can.

"Where's Bongani?" Todd asked.

Dan looked up, swallowing the sausage in his mouth. "Doing a quick scout of the area."

Todd reached for his rifle and got to his feet. "Well, that's great. Money we're paying him, and he comes and goes as he pleases. Some guide he's turning out to be."

"Well, I think it's good. I wouldn't want to run into any dangerous animals if I didn't have to."

"This is Africa, Dan. Everything here is dangerous."

Todd sat next to his friend.

"Do you want what's left of the sausages?" Dan asked.

"No, thanks."

Dan pulled his sleeves down. His skin was noticeably fair, even at night. "So what culture is Bongani from?"

"Well, Zulu originally, but I'm not sure, to be honest. He's a bit of a rogue. He can speak many of the languages around here, and he's done all sorts of work all round Africa, which is what matters."

"Ah, okay."

Staring into the distance, Todd shook his right leg. It was never easy to calm the current that pulsated throughout his body when he was on a job, and this was deadly work after all. Poaching was a serious offense in Southern Africa. They wouldn't be the first to get into a firefight with the park rangers. On top of that, you never knew what wildlife you could run into.

"Did he say how long he'd be?" Todd asked.

"Nope."

The three of them had been dropped off near one of the national park's borders. On foot, they had entered through a weak spot in the fence. They then dashed deep into the park, where there would be less patrols than on the perimeter. They left all electronics behind, fearful any instruments could be used to locate them.

"Well, I guess we ought to be preparing for the night," Todd said. "These tents aren't going to put themselves up. Trust Bongani to miss all the work."

"He said to wait until he checked out the area."

"You got to be kidding me. Who is paying who here?"

Dan kept quiet.

"Come on now, up. Let's get this shit going. I'm not gonna wait until Bongani has finished dancing to some ancestor so he can sleep comfortably."

Dan stumbled after Todd.

"You all right there?" Todd asked, reaching into his large backpack.

"Yeah, the old right knee takes a few moments to warm up."

After an hour there was still no sign of Bongani. Todd and Dan had erected all the tents, checked their gear, and prepared a cold meal for Bongani's return. The two sat with legs outstretched as they gazed at the sky. They inhaled the dusty, dry atmosphere of the barren world around them.

"Where the hell is he?" Todd mumbled.

"Being thorough, I hope."

Todd chuckled. "Bongani is a pro. He'll be fine. I'm more worried he's gone and taken a snooze in a tree. Anyway, I told you this isn't like our excursions into Asia. You better have what it takes to do this."

"I—"

The patter of feet on the hard soil stopped Dan from defending the weight he had gained the last few months. Bongani appeared, running toward the two men. He came at such a speed that he didn't have time to slow down and toppled over one of the tents.

Bongani was back up in a flash. "We have to go now."

Todd frowned. "Why? We just got everything sorted."

"That does not matter. The rangers are coming." Bongani moved for his backpack and filled it with any items near him. He zipped it closed, lifted it onto his back, and started jogging.

Todd looked around, considering if he should try to pack one of the tents, but a low humming sound stopped him. The sound got louder.

"Fuck," Todd said. "Get your bag, Dan. We're going to have to run."

"And all the stuff?"

"That's a chopper coming." Todd grabbed his pack and ran after Bongani. Their guide moved fast with considerable ease.

Dan eventually caught up with them, but by then the chopper's blades sounded like a whirlpool in the sky.

Todd peered back and saw a spotlight shining down. More lights shone in the blackness behind them. "I count three vehicles with the chopper."

"We're fucked," Dan said. "Holy shit, we're fucked."

"Calm down, you fool. Bongani, what are our chances?"

"Better if we run faster." Bongani picked up the pace.

Todd lost track of time. He kept a steady pace as they pressed on, motivated by the lack of noise, especially the fading chopper. Even the shrubs that would wrap around his feet and the bigger stones tipping his balance couldn't slow him down. He sensed the three of them were getting away from the rangers. Bongani seemed to agree and eventually slacked off the pace. Dan, wheezing a few feet behind Todd, was audibly thankful when they hit a jog.

Bongani stopped.

Todd took the moment to regulate his breathing and heard Dan panting; Bongani seemed fine. The stars in the sky provided decent illumination, but Todd wanted a better idea of where they were. He switched on the only flashlight they had taken during the escape and shined its beam around the area. There were some low-growing bushes close by and a few trees around them farther on.

"We shall rest here," Bongani said.

Dan plopped down on the ground. "Thank goodness."

"What you thinking, Bongani? Did we lose them?" Todd asked.

"Hard to say. Maybe."

"That all you gonna give me, mister expert?"

"We should rest. Tomorrow will be a long day."

Todd waved Bongani off and went to sit next to Dan. He hated the fact that they had lost so much gear, especially as he was the one who'd fronted the costs. His mind kept active as he lay on the hard soil and stared at the sky. He needed to find a way to salvage the operation.

"*Lala kahle,*" Bongani said in Zulu.

Todd ignored him. He didn't want to say good night back. If Bongani hadn't walked to scout the area, maybe the rangers wouldn't have found them.

* * *

Morning brought a clear cerulean sky. Todd swore at his jacket, which had been his makeshift bed. It had done nothing to soften the hard African ground. There was no breeze to caress his senses, and he continued his curses at the prospect of the forthcoming hot, dry day. Why did he do this kind of work? As he got older the gnawing guilt within grew stronger, as he knew this wasn't the work of a good person. He had a wife and young child. They needed him around and not in a jail cell somewhere. They also needed money, and this work was what Todd knew.

He tapped Dan on the shoulder. "Ten minutes."

Dan, with his arms wrapped over his head, didn't reply.

Todd stood, stretched, and wandered off to a heap of rocks about twenty yards from where they had slept. Bongani was using one of the flatter-shaped rocks as a seat. He gazed across the veld and spoke without turning around to face Todd.

"*Sawubona*, Mister Watson."

"Morning, Bongani."

"*Unjani?*"

"I've been better. How are you?"

"Same, but I am alive, and that means I can change my situation."

Todd shrugged. "Great, so let's get real. How bad is it? Are we fucked?"

"No. The land can provide, and the wrong animals we can avoid. It is the rangers we will have to be watchful for, especially as they likely will have found the gear. That may have been what gave us the time to escape, but it will also have sent them into red alert."

"But the wildlife? If we can't avoid them, that is, we have one rifle between us, not a lot of ammo, and one panga."

"Do not worry." Bongani tossed a stone into a bush a few feet from him. "The wrong animals I can keep us away from. I told you. As for what you really want to know but do not ask, my acquaintances and I have done the job before with much less."

Todd turned back to Dan. There was still no sign of movement. He spat on the dusty earth. "Good to hear, Bongani."

When Dan awoke, the men shared a bag of nuts and a tin of beans, then set off on the next part of their mission. Bongani was confident he knew where the rhinos liked to graze during the day. However, he had warned them it was an arduous journey. The previous night had seen them run in the wrong direction from their objective. Todd wasn't worried about the distance. His dilemma was the limited arsenal at their disposal, but he was desperate to come away with something. The once ten-day-long planned haul had turned into a three-day hit-and-run.

* * *

The walk was mundane. Apart from the occasional shift away from the odd pack of animals, which Bongani knew by checking for tracks, there wasn't much activity or any sightings of anything. The terrain also didn't offer much in terms of view. Todd grew tired of the same prickly bushes, loose stones, and sharp thorn trees. Bongani, however, had become more agitated as the day moved on, eventually mumbling to himself. Todd couldn't resist prying.

"Bongani, is something troubling you?"

Bongani stopped. He got onto his haunches, almost as if he were checking for tracks again, and moved some of the soil around. "Something is not right."

"What?"

"I am not sure, but I have heard stories of this."

"Stories of what?" Todd held his hands up.

"The landscape is not how it should be. And the smell, it is ashy, almost like the air after a fire. I fear we have entered an old realm. On one of my trips I heard a *sangoma* speak much of this."

"What's a *sangoma*?" Dan asked.

"They're traditional healers," Todd said. "But also, they're meant to be able to speak to spirits or gods, protect their people, and fight evil. If you believe that shit."

"It is not shit," Bongani said.

"Bongani, has the sun gotten to you? Great. Just what we need: our guide is going nuts from heatstroke."

"No, I am fine. This problem is real. I have not encountered it before, but I know we must keep on until we get back into our world."

Todd placed his hand on his forehead. "Yeah, yeah. Let's get back to our world before the aliens arrive."

"Try not to look around too much. If you see or hear anything odd, keep moving. You do not notice anything, and hopefully, nothing notices you."

Dan shook his head. "No, no, no. That's too creepy."

"Oh, please," Todd said. "The rangers, now, they're what we have to be worried about and not some mumbo jumbo of being lost in some old realm. Hell, what's next? Dinosaurs?"

Bongani stood. His temples strained as he walked ahead. "Do as I say, please, and we should be fine."

Todd labored forward. Bongani's strange tale couldn't prevent the trek from becoming monotonous again. The hot sun burned his face as his eyes grew tired. He jolted when Dan tapped his shoulder.

"What?"

"Check over there." Dan pointed to their left.

There was a strange little tree, all on its own, in the middle of nowhere. The tree was unlike any Todd had seen in the park with its large lush leaves, its thick chocolate-colored trunk, and the bright green grass growing around it. A red orb-like light shimmered above the tree, almost as if the light was a portal that had transplanted the tree from another dimension. That was nonsense of course. Some mundane phenomena probably caused the red light's appearance. Still, the tree had an allure in the otherwise predictable environment.

"Come on, let's check it out," Todd said.

The two men jogged to the tree and found peculiar oval-shaped purple fruits hanging from its branches. They looked juicy and had a sweet aroma. The saliva ran in Todd's mouth; Dan picked one of the fruits.

"*Aikona, aikona.*" Bongani ran to them. "No, no, no, we do not eat this."

Dan didn't release the fruit.

Bongani slapped it out of his hand. "*Hamba, hamba.*"

"What the hell is it?" Todd asked. "Is it poisonous, Bongani?"

"No, but it is not of our time. We must leave this tree alone. I believe it is the source of seeing that which has passed. Very bad, very bad. You do not wish to see such things. You do not wish to invite such things to see you. Come now, you are wasting time. You do not listen. We must keep moving forward to get back to our time. Do you want to be stuck here forever? You never know when these realms open or close."

"Are the fruits some kind of hallucinogenic?"

"No, what you see is real. But you waste time with such questions. Come now, okay?"

Todd gave him a thumbs-up, faking agreement. Bongani had said it wasn't poisonous and it wasn't a hallucinogenic. That was good enough for him. As soon as Bongani walked ahead, he turned to Dan and indicated for him to snatch some of the fruits. Dan duly obliged and picked a few of the juiciest-looking ones, then hid them in his pack.

The two men caught up with Bongani, who had increased the pace again. Todd felt a slight bit of concern regarding Bongani, as the heat could do strange things to a person. His story of an old realm and then the reaction to the tree didn't sit right.

Todd was glad he carried the rifle.

* * *

They were covering decent ground when Todd became annoyed by the stiffness in his neck. He massaged the lower right side and looked up. At first, he assumed there was something wrong with his eyesight as the sky appeared to have a light purple shimmer. He blinked and focused. The strange color remained.

"The sky is..." Dan said.

"Purple," Todd added. "Probably some phenomenon, like—"

"Huh," Bongani interrupted. "No phenomenon I know of. This is old times. We are still not in our time."

Todd looked at Dan, shaking his head.

The sky did change color again, this time to a light gray. Dusk had fallen. They'd been walking the entire day and had found no food or water. With their supplies at a critical low, this was fast becoming a serious problem.

Bongani stopped.

"What's it now?" Todd asked.

"Shhh." Bongani placed his index finger over his mouth.

Dull *thud*s echoed when all was still. They weren't random; they had a pattern. One dull *thud* came, and then two quicker *thuds*. It could be animals on the march? Todd quickly ceased the idea as nonsense. The sound was too rhythmic. It had a beat.

"Drums?" Dan asked.

Bongani nodded. "Come, come. We must move away quick."

"But who the hell would be playing drums out here?" Todd asked.

He got no reply. Bongani jogged at a quick pace. Infuriated, Todd bolted after him. He was about to physically push on their guide when he saw the landscape ahead was changing. There were trees and bushes that he recalled belonging in this part of Africa. To his left, he even thought he saw two giraffes in the distance, but with night almost upon them, he wasn't sure.

Bongani stopped again, got to his knees, and picked up some of the soil. Slowly, he let it fall from his hand. He took off his backpack and dropped it next to him. It wasn't quite a smile, but a brief grin appeared over his face. Todd noted it was the first time Bongani looked relaxed since mentioning the old realm.

"We have made it," Bongani said. "We are back in our time."

"Great." Todd decided not to ask Bongani who could make drum sounds out here. He assumed the sounds were yet another phenomenon of the wild, but he had to admit on some level it was a bit odd. He had been to different parts of Africa on many occasions, but this was the first time he'd seen purple skies shimmering overhead or heard drums in the middle of a protected animal park.

"We will have to camp here tonight. We will only get to the rhino tomorrow, thanks to the old realm wasting our time."

"Sounds like a plan, I guess." Todd frowned. How good of a guide was Bongani, truly? He'd come highly recommended by some people who had ventured into the country on "special" trips. Yet Todd couldn't shake the idea that he had spun the tale of the old realm to cover for not knowing his way around, which led them to spend an entire day searching for the rhinos. Secondly, they hadn't come across water, and the only fruit they'd discovered had caused a strange reaction from Bongani.

Bongani patted his chest. "I shall keep first watch, and you two can get some rest. I will scout the area a bit first. Do not worry."

"You want some food before you go?" Dan asked. "We still got an energy bar or two and some snacks."

"No, not now. You two eat and rest."

Bongani headed out into landscape held firmly in the grip of night.

Todd and Dan ate an energy bar and drank some water. With no tents or sleeping bags, they had to try and find spots on the ground that were level and as soft as possible. Only conversation and the stars above were their entertainment. Their chat didn't last long, as both men were tired from the long day. The stars held their gazes as eyelids became heavy.

The roar of an engine startled Todd. The sound was impressive in the still night air, and he sprang up, ready for action. It was too dark to see what was coming their way. He grabbed the rifle; Dan, also up, took the panga. They huddled behind a nearby bush.

Bongani shouted in the distance.

As he neared, Todd could make out his distant silhouette. "If that fool has brought the rangers to us again, I swear I'm shooting him."

"What's he saying?" Dan asked.

"Fuck knows, but I hear the engine coming closer."

"Wait, I think he said Jimmy or get-gym-ga."

"*Gijima*?"

"Yeah, that's it. What's it mean?"

"Run."

A gunshot, close by, invaded the night. Both men grabbed what they could and ran. Todd turned his neck to glance at what unfolded behind them. Bongani appeared to stand still, but then he dropped to the ground. Bright floodlights on a vehicle switched on and illuminated the spot where their guide had fallen.

"What happened?" Dan asked.

"Don't look. Keep running."

"Where are we going?"

"Not sure. I think it's the way we came."

"What are we going to do?"

"Just fucking run."

"We're running away from the rhino again."

"Dan, you idiot. They shot Bongani."

* * *

There was no escape from the heat as both men ran into the night. Perspiration poured down their faces as their pace slowed due to exhaustion. They found the bushes and loose rocks underfoot more treacherous, and both had fallen once or twice during their getaway. It was harder without a guide ahead of them. Why did the rangers have to shoot Bongani? Sure, his skills appeared to be all over the place as a guide, but he had been a good person at heart. He could've learned and improved. Todd resisted any more sadness with ease, as he had done many times before.

He shined his flashlight every now and again and noticed that the wildlife and plant life waned once more. This time there were no drums and the sky didn't change color. Todd assumed they would find the clearing that Bongani had called the center of the old realm. He didn't believe in such myths and legends, but he didn't like the idea of being too out in the open. It took away any shelter or cover but could aid the speed of their escape. He scanned his sides.

"Here," Todd said, shining his flashlight at some nearby bushes. "Let's stop here. We'll take a quick break. If we hear the rangers, we keep moving."

"I don't hear the vehicles anymore."

"Yeah."

"Poor Bongani. Why would they shoot him?"

Todd kicked at the ground beneath his feet. "Fuck knows, maybe he resisted arrest. Maybe he attacked one of them. All I know is I wouldn't want to be apprehended in this shithole."

Dan nodded, taking a seat on the ground.

"What we got to eat?" Todd asked.

Dan searched through his bag. "A protein bar, a can of beans, and a bag of nuts—oh, and four of those strange fruits."

"Fuck it, let's try one of them."

Todd ripped open one of the peculiar fruits. It didn't smell off, nor did it smell like peaches or almonds, which was a good sign. He placed some of the juice on his finger; he saw and felt no irritation. Todd put some of the juice on his lips. It didn't burn. The taste was sweet, so sweet he couldn't resist licking his lips.

"Good enough for me." Todd took a bite.

Both men ate. The fruit burst with flavor. It was exactly what they required, and energy surged through Todd's body. The world around him seemed brighter, clearer.

"Damn, that was good," Dan said. "Seconds?"

"No, we should keep the other two in case we don't find anything for a while. It's safe to say this operation has been a bust. I'll have to worry about the lost cash when we get back. At least we won't have to pay Bongani his other half." Todd curled his hand into a fist. "What a wasteful expense he turned out to be. We need to get the fuck out of here."

"Yeah..."

"We'll have to keep going back until we find a perimeter fence."

Dan stood, rocking from side to side.

"You all right?" Todd asked.

"Yeah, yeah. Just a bit groggy."

"Must be the heat."

They decided to press on through the night. The call of home and the boost from the fruit now fueled their muscles. After a while, Todd thought he could see the clearing they had passed earlier in the day. He loathed having to traverse it, but they had no other choice, so he carried on, only to feel Dan pull on him.

"What the hell, man?"

"Wow. Look over there. Don't you see them?"

Todd strained his eyes under the starry sky. He saw nothing but the emptiness of the clearing ahead. "What do you see?"

"There are animals everywhere."

"This isn't a time for jokes."

"I'm not joking. There are elephants, giraffes, zebras, gazelles, and so much more. But they look odd, a bit hazy, and they all have a blue shimmer." Dan stepped forward. "I want to see them closer."

Todd reached for his friend, who pulled free from the grip. "Wait, Dan. I think you're tripping. I feel fine, so it's not the fruit. Must be from the sun earlier. You need to take a breather and get some water."

Dan didn't listen. He upped his pace and jogged into the clearing, heading for its center.

Todd shook his head while keeping his distance from Dan, deciding to let his delusions play out—so long as he was quiet. There were no signs of lights anywhere around them. He could only hope the rangers had quit for the night.

"Rhinos," Dan said. "Todd, there are rhinos here, and they're everywhere."

"Okay, Dan. Take it easy now. You sure you don't want some water?"

"They're circling me, and one is coming forward."

"You're having a bad trip. Relax." Todd decided enough was enough. He marched to Dan. His plan was to get his friend to sit and have some water.

Dan lifted off the ground, his body flying backward like a rag doll. At first, Todd thought he was hallucinating as well, but when Dan crashed back to the ground, the truth of their current situation hit him hard.

"What the fuck?" Todd ran to his friend's aid.

Dan was inert. Todd tried talking to him, but he got no reply. He shined the flashlight over his friend and saw the blood pooling all around him. Icy tendrils shot down his spine. He rolled Dan onto his back, gasping as he saw the massive hole in his chest. He checked Dan's vitals, and the truth surfaced.

He was dead.

Todd looked around, seeking someone or something to blame. He was confused, and his mind thundered as he tried to find a tether to reality, but he remained stuck, grasping at liquid thoughts. A large shadow moved in his peripheral vision. As he turned his head, a rhino-like shape disappeared into the darkness.

"Come back, you fuck."

Another form moved to his right. Todd turned in time to see a shape like the first headed for him. Before the impact, he glimpsed the animal. It was a rhino. The beast, adorned in a sparkling powder-blue coating, lowered its head and aimed its horn at him. The rhino vanished, but Todd sensed the impact was coming. His body lifted into the air as a magnificent force struck him.

Everything went dark when he hit the ground.

* * *

Todd awoke, rattled. He sat up, realizing he must have passed out. Fragmented images shot up in the fore of his mind. How many of them had been real? He figured the fruit must have been some hallucinogenic after all, and a warmth rose in his core. If it was all a bad trip, Dan was alive.

Footsteps approached from behind him.

"Dan?"

"No, I am not Dan," someone said.

Todd turned around. The short dark man before him wore a strange and colorful ensemble. A feather stuck out from some band on his head, there were colorful beads on his arms, and a type of animal-skin loincloth covered him. He held a walking stick with a large ball at its top. The man seemed calm as he stared at Todd.

"Who are you? What do you want? Where am I?" The questions shot out of Todd's mouth in quick-fire succession, surprising him.

"I am a *sangoma*. I wanted to communicate with a certain old one. You are in the old realm."

"What? What's going on? I want to get out of here. Where's Dan?"

"Dead one, you ask many questions. It is not necessary anymore. I do not know what you have done to anger the old ones, but there is nothing that can be done for you. As for your Dan, I fear he is dead. They may have allowed him to move on to a different realm to see out the times. You, they have not."

"Why do you keep calling me 'dead one'?"

The *sangoma* looked to the sky. "Do you see the sun?"

Todd looked to the heavens. "No, I don't. What the fuck? Where is it? Tell me now. What trickery is this?"

"For you, the sun is gone. You have died, and recently. Soon the blue skies you have known will also fade. You will wander these empty lands under the purple skies. It is best to accept it. I feel for you. It is not a nice way to spend eternity, away from others passed, even for one who has angered the old ones. Though, you will have many animals for company."

"I'm sick of this mumbo-jumbo bullshit. Fuck you and all your so-called old ones. I'm out of here."

"You will never be able to leave the sound of the drums. They are a protection we have put to stop anything coming through into our time. I am afraid that the drums are the border of your world now, dead one."

Todd waved off the *sangoma* and walked ahead. The anger rose within him as he tried to determine how much he truly loathed Africa. He turned around to launch some more choice words at the *sangoma.*

The man was gone.

Todd heard an oncoming vehicle. It was most likely the park rangers, but he had endured enough and decided to give himself up. As they approached, he put his hands over his head. Instead of driving toward him, the rangers stopped a couple hundred yards ahead. All three of the men in the vehicle got out. They searched the land.

"Hey, over here," Todd shouted.

No response came, and he jogged to them.

He heard them talking, but he couldn't make out what they said. The words sounded as if they were coming through a distorting old radio. He walked to one of the rangers and patted him on the back. His hand went through the man, and Todd found himself toppling forward onto the ground.

"What the fuck is going on?"

The men ignored him, and one of them picked up Todd's rifle.

Todd focused as hard as he could to try and understand what the men were saying. He heard broken parts here and there.

"...all three are dead..."

"...body was found over...vehicle now..."

"What the fuck are you talking about?" Todd made his way to the back of their vehicle, a dusty, well-used pickup. He investigated the back. There was a blanket over a concealed shape. The shape, Todd realized, was that of a body.

"Is it Dan? Bongani? You assholes, what have you done?"

Todd used all the might he could muster, which was barely enough to lift a side of the blanket off the corpse, or had a bit of wind helped? Either way, it sufficed. He could see the face. It didn't belong to either Dan or Bongani.

It was his.

He stood motionless as the men got into the pickup and drove off. Realizing he needed to do something, he ran after them. He screamed, swore, and begged for them to stop. Confusion enveloped him. Fear flooded within.

Todd ran into an invisible wall and toppled backward. The sounds of the drums came. At first, they were soft, but they continued to get louder. Todd's head threatened to explode. He kept retreating, eventually losing all track of time and distance. When the drums were a faint tapping sound, he stopped.

The sky had returned to the peculiar shade of purple. Looking around, Todd determined he was back in the center of the old realm's clearing. He saw the animals that Dan had seen. They all sparkled blue as they made their way over the landscape. Somehow, he knew every one of them was dead and that they were now ghosts of the past. They were living out eternity, grazing and wandering, as they had done their entire lives.

Todd looked at his hands.
They sparkled blue.

THE DESTROYER

Nafretiri ran across the desert, ignoring the anxiety of traversing the expansive terrain at dusk. The village was in her wake. She upped her pace, battling the loose silver sands beneath her bare feet. After the bad boys had cornered her by the lake the first time, she'd promised herself she would never again cower in fear or—even worse—cry. Their teasing this evening had tested her resolve. Fortunately, she had escaped their clutches before they could break her. All she needed now was a moment to find equilibrium.

A nearby dune promised refuge.

Something peculiar stood out about the small dune. Even in the fading light, Nafretiri could see its shape appeared unnatural. She wasn't surprised to spot the large stones peeking out on its sides. The stones reminded her of those used for the pyramids or for the buildings in the capital. The wind that had blown earlier must have exposed them.

At the top, she didn't see anything but desert sand. The rest of the structure likely remained buried below. She wiped perspiration from her brow as the heat from the day smothered the land. Inhaling the dry, dusty air, she sat and looked at her village in the distance. Her people were one of the pockets of resistance that had scattered into the desert. They were tired of the cruel, oppressive rule of the pharaoh, whose law was most harsh in the main towns and the villages on the floodplains along the Nile. Her people sought to start a better way of life.

When they found the oasis in the middle of nowhere beneath the unrelenting sun, they had at first decided to rest for a few days. The oasis, with its small lake, trees, and lush vegetation, kept providing. They had water, shelter, and means to make fire. Even the odd animals and critters seemed to pop up from time to time. The elders said that their people, chosen and blessed, dare not leave such a gift, and it didn't take long for the people to call the oasis home.

Nafretiri reached back with her arm, running her hand through the sand. She flinched when her fingers encountered a hard object. Turning around, Nafretiri saw that it was another stone, except this one was darker. She moved some of the sand away and was amazed to see the stone was as black as night, and there were markings—golden hieroglyphics—carved into its surface. As Nafretiri moved more sand away, she realized that the stone must be a part of the structure, but it was smaller, much smaller than the stones she'd seen protruding on the dune's side.

She cursed when her attempt to move the stone failed.

The stone was wedged between two of the larger, light-brown stones; Nafretiri gripped it tighter. She wanted it and pulled with all her might. The stone refused to budge.

"I wouldn't do that," a weak, dry voice said from her left.

Nafretiri whipped her head around. A strange man stood in the gray world. He wore a hooded white cloak and held a gold scepter in his hand. His face remained hidden by the hood and the dark shadow it created.

Nafretiri rose to her feet. "Who are you? Where did you come from?"

"I have come from nowhere and everywhere. The desert in which you wander is part of my domain."

"I do not recognize you."

"I am Set. Do you truly not know of your gods?"

Nafretiri shook her head. "Not really. Our village doesn't follow the old ways anymore. Why can't I move the stone?"

"That stone is what keeps the arch of life open for this part of the desert. Without it, the arch would collapse. Now tell me, young girl, is your lack of understanding of your gods why your face looks the way it does?"

"No. I—I was in a fight."

"I hope you battled some beast and were victorious, but I somehow doubt that, considering you can't even move a pebble."

"The stone is much bigger than a pebble, and it was not a beast I battled. Hemiunu, Kheruef, and Sebni—three boys from my village—attacked me. I fought them off."

"Ha! You are a poor liar. I already know what happened to you. I saw it all." He waved his hand. "Why did you not kill them for attacking you? Why did you run away like a coward?"

"I—"

Set held his hand up. "The time for excuses has passed. Egypt needs strong men and women. An empire of cowards led by a weak pharaoh is destined to fall. If it costs us the lives of a thousand weak ones in exchange for one that is strong, it would be worth it. Your village is full of cowards. Do you wish to stay in your village forever? As a coward? A slave?"

"We are free!"

"You are a fool. You and your people hide from the weakest pharaoh ever known, a shame to the great dynasties of the past. You can't even fend for yourself!" He pulled a pouch out from the cloak he wore. The pouch made a clinking sound, and Nafretiri knew it must contain coins or something even more precious.

"Show me that you can be a strong Egyptian woman." Set smiled. "And then this gold is yours. With it you can start a new life wherever you want to go. You can be your own person. You will have power and freedom."

Nafretiri gazed at the pouch Set held before her. He had untied it, giving Nafretiri a clear view of its contents. She had all but forgotten about the peculiar black stone, for the twinkling gold in the pouch mesmerized her. She'd never had a choice on calling the oasis home. Older people had decided. She'd dreamed many a night of what the major cities were like. The gold could provide the means to leave the oasis, and its pull was unlike anything she had ever felt.

"What must I do?"

Set put the pouch away. When his hand came out from the cloak, it held a curved blade.

Nafretiri flinched, stepping backward.

"Do not be afraid. If you are to be your own person, it is an emotion you can no longer have. Do you understand?"

Nafretiri nodded.

"Good. Now, are you ready to do the task that will give you your freedom?"

"I—"

Set took a step forward. "Will you live in fear forever?"

Nafretiri shook her head.

"Then tell me, are you ready?"

"Yes," she said, accepting the blade. "What must I do with it?"

Set lifted his hood off. Nafretiri took a step back. Seeing the dark curved snout, the long rectangular ears, the empty eyes—focused on her—and the tufts of copper-colored fur around the strange animal-like head caused a frigid chill to grip her chest. She wondered if it was not some weird mask the man wore, because she could see that the man had normal human hands. A part of her doubted it.

"Bring me the head of the large one, the leader, Hemiunu," Set boomed. His voice was sonorous. Gone was the dry, crackling voice Nafretiri had first heard. "I want the hands of his minions, Kheruef and Sebni, as well. Then, you shall have proven yourself. And then you shall receive your reward."

"I must kill?"

"Have you failed already? Do you not wish to claim your reward?"

"I have not failed yet. And yes, I do, I do want the reward." Nafretiri battled to steady the blade in her shaking hands. The newfound voice along with the true image of an angered Set was a potent combination.

Set put his hood back on, much to the relief of Nafretiri. "I will be here with your gold when you return. Do not fail me, Nafretiri, daughter of Egypt."

"I won't," Nafretiri said, trying to act unconcerned that Set knew her name when she hadn't given it to him. She turned and headed back down the strange dune, narrowing in on the lights of her village while trying to sort through all the thoughts racing in her mind.

She didn't turn back to see if Set was watching.

* * *

Nafretiri came to a decision before she was home. The boys were terrible people, especially Hemiunu. She would bring justice, not murder. She consoled herself with the fact that she was saving many from suffering at the hands of Hemiunu. Fueled by the desire to experience more than the life the village offered, her logic made sense, but she was unsure how she would accomplish the tasks Set had given her. Stalking between the huts, she knew cutting off Hemiunu's head would be the hardest, so she left the hands of Kheruef and Sebni for last.

Fortune favored Nafretiri; Hemiunu was snoring on the softened floor right near the entrance of his family's hut. His parents and brother slept farther inside their home, which smelled of perspiration and spices. If Hemiunu screamed, the entire village would be alerted to Nafretiri's actions. When she reached Kheruef and Sebni, she would need to bind and gag them before cutting off their right hands, but as she knelt beside Hemiunu, it dawned on her that she didn't need to take the same precautions with him. She just needed to make sure the first strike brought death.

Nafretiri held the tip of the blade over Hemiunu's heart. Her free hand was above his mouth, ready to clasp down if he uttered a sound. She would pierce the vital organ, killing Hemiunu, and then cut off his head without the worry of any noise or actions. She hoped it would be as easy as she had learned to do on other animals. Time was of the essence, because the potent copper smell of blood could alert the rest of the family, even if she was quiet. Steadying her nerves, Nafretiri tightened her grip around the blade. A strange current flooded her limbs, forcing her muscles to contract. She couldn't move.

Thoughts banged on the walls of her mind.

What was she doing?

She couldn't answer.

Something within her told her this was not the right thing to do. It was not the right way to achieve her dreams. She could see the gold vanishing, piece by piece. Feeling both relief and despair, she slunk out of the hut.

She would face Set and tell him she wasn't interested in his deal. She would tell him she had chosen not to kill and that she would sort out the bullies her own way, even if it meant being stuck in the village, poor and miserable for a few more years.

One day she would find a better way out.

* * *

Up the dune Nafretiri went. She stepped over the strange black stone, now uncovered. Set sat, staring at the heavens, as if he had not a care in the world. Nafretiri blinked to be sure that the seat she saw beneath Set—a crocodile—was true. The beast lay comfortably with its master on top.

Nafretiri didn't wish to get too close. The apprehension she'd felt making her way from her village had become more severe as it moved from a trickle to a steady flow throughout her body. With force of will, she ceased her fearful thoughts. She knew she couldn't show any type of fear toward Set. It was best to be straightforward so that the ominous stranger would be on his way.

"I see you do not carry anything but the clean blade I gave you. I was hoping to see blood." Set tapped the bottom of his scepter on the earth.

"I've decided to pass on your offer," she said. "I do not wish to kill, and I will handle my problems my own way. I will also find my own gold."

"That is unacceptable." Set ran his hand over the scales of the crocodile's back. The animal moved its head to the side, peering toward Nafretiri.

"Will you command your beast to kill me now?" she asked, readying the blade at her side.

"No, I will not," Set said, shaking his head. "Death will teach you nothing."

"Then what? I have told you I am not interested in your deal. You should be off now...and take your beast with you."

"Are you brave now? I will be on my way. If—and only if—you can pull out that black stone you were admiring earlier."

Nafretiri glanced back at the stone. "But you warned me not to do it. You said that it keeps something open and—"

"Hush! If you are too afraid and too weak, I guess I will not be leaving. It is a pleasant night after all. I rather like it here."

Nafretiri wanted the man gone. She walked back to the black stone and knelt, seeking a strong grip on the stone with her hands. Pulling on it at first seemed to do nothing, but she noticed a small shift on one side of the stone as she tried again. She focused her energy and strength, and the stone budged. An odd current ran from her extremities to her core as she kept hold of the stone—or had she only imagined it?

When the stone was almost free, it seemed harder to pull on, but she persevered. She was so close. Ignoring the sweat that now drenched her, the burning in her arms, and the pain in her forehead from all the concentration, Nafretiri gave one mighty tug.

The stone came free.

She dropped it at her feet.

The two large brown stones, which the black stone had separated, moved toward each other, slowly at first, then finally came together, erasing the space between them. She braced herself for a reaction from the dune.

Time slowed.

"Nothing is happening," Nafretiri said. "Now you can be gone. I did what you said."

"I will be off. But remember, Nafretiri. You brought this lesson upon yourself. I warned you that Egypt needs only strong people. You could have done this the easier way with the punishment of the three that hurt you."

Thunder boomed in the clear skies.

Nafretiri asked, "What is happening?"

"I did not lie when I told you that stone was important." Set pointed toward her village.

A strange, wind-like sound exploded all around Nafretiri, as if someone were breathing in through clenched teeth yet amplified a thousand times. She turned toward her home, narrowing her eyes. The sands had turned into a whirlpool, sucking in the lake, and along with the lake, the vegetation and the huts. Down they went, below the surface of the desert. Nafretiri's heart writhed in pain as she watched her family, her friends, the other villagers, and even the three boys who bullied her disappear into the earth. It was a horror she struggled to bear witness to. Her breath vacated her lungs.

A spell of dizziness overcame her. Then...

Calm settled on the world.

The whirlpool of sand returned to its usual self. Silence fell over the void of what had once been an oasis seen as a gift. Nothing, not even a speck of grass or drop of water, remained to suggest that it had once ever been there.

"What have you done?" Nafretiri asked, turning with the blade ready to strike.

Like the oasis and her village, Set was gone, as was the crocodile. Alongside her lay the black stone, but all the golden markings had vanished.

Nafretiri ran down the dune.

She headed to the center of what had once been her village and knelt on the soft, shifting sands, remembering the promise she'd made to herself: she would never cry or cower in fear again. She gripped the handle of the blade tight and braced through her emotions. When they had passed, she stood and calculated which direction would take her to the capital. The heart of the pharaoh's reign was her destination. If she could not cut down Set, the god who had tricked her and destroyed her world, she would take down the pharaoh who allowed the worshipping of such gods.

Nafretiri no longer sought gold or glory. She wished now to be only a ghost—a ghost who dealt in pain and misery. Everyone would pay. The people who allowed such pharaohs and gods to reign would run for their lives. When their future generations returned, they would look at the broken pyramids and wonder who had built them and for what purpose. They would see the fallen cities of the pharaohs and speculate as to what had brought about their destruction. The gods would be nothing but dusty tales; they would lose their shine and relevance as time moved on without them.

Nafretiri would have revenge for her family and for her people, and to do this she would need to erase a dynasty, topple the gods, and send a nation's people fleeing. She would start small, like a grain of sand, but in the end, she would create her own whirlpool that would swallow her enemies.

She would not fail.

"I am no longer Nafretiri," she said to the sands of Egypt. "I am no longer the scared girl of the village." She lifted her blade to the sky. "I am the *destroyer*."